PRAISE FOR
Revolt *of the* Animals:

"Levy's book has the vision and compassion of *Mrs. Frisby and the Rats of NIMH* and other great animal fantasies for grown-ups of every age. With insight and humor it reminds us – and alas, we need reminding – that nuclear and environmental hazards threaten all animals, not just humans."

~Jonathan Balcombe, Ph.D., author of *Second Nature: The Inner Lives of Animals* and *Pleasurable Kingdom*

"Levy captures the grave realities of present-day world conflicts while artfully weaving a story of hope – hope for the continuance of life on earth *in spite of* the humans, and *because of* the dedicated vigilance of the animals."

~ Steve Ann Chambers, former president, Animal Legal Defense Fund

"The animals get it. This book shows why. Recommended reading for people of all ages who care about the environment and the planet."

~Jeffrey Moussaieff Masson, Ph.D., author of *The Face on the Plate* and *When Elephants Weep*

"David Levy's characterization of the animals is engaging and convincing – maybe our animal associates are going to help us escape self-destruction! Old Eddie, an elephant at the National Zoo, is particularly effective."

~ Carolivia Herron, Ph.D., author of *Nappy Hair* and *Always an Olivia*

"Terrorists have hatched plans to start a nuclear war, and only the animal kingdom, led by enterprising elephants, turtles, electric rays, and an odiferous stink bug—to name but a few!—can put a stop to it. In this wild-ride-of-a-fable, the follies of mankind are seen anew through the perceptions and sensibilities of 'less sophisticated' creatures of the world."

~William Loizeaux, author of *Clarence Cochran, a Human Boy* and *Wings*

ADDITIONAL BOOKS BY THE AUTHOR:

The Potomac Conspiracy

The Best Parent Is Both Parents: A Guide to Shared Parenting in the 21st Century (Editor)

Creating a Safer Society: 10 Ways to Help Children Avoid Crime, Drugs, Teenage Pregnancy, and Drugs (2011)

Revolt *of the* Animals

[illegible]

Nov- 2010

Revolt

of the Animals

A NOVEL *by*

DAVID L. LEVY

Earth Home Publishing
HYATTSVILLE, MD

Revolt of the Animals: A Novel
by David L. Levy,
published by Earth Home Publishing, Hyattsville, MD.

Earth Home Publishing
P.O Box 5282, Hyattsville, MD 20782
davidlevy2@gmail.com
http://earthhomepublishers.org/

Illustration on front cover, chapter pages and page 11 courtesy of "SAVAGE ©"

Cover and Interior Design & Layout by Brian Taylor, Pneuma Books, LLC
For more info on Pneuma Books, visit www.pneumabooks.com

Publisher's Cataloging-in-Publication Data
(Prepared by The Donohue Group)

Levy, David L.
Revolt of the animals : a novel / by David L. Levy.

p. : ill. ; cm.

ISBN: 978-0-9828285-2-6 (hardcover)

ISBN: 978-0-9828285-0-2 (pbk.)

1. Terrorism--Prevention--Congresses--Fiction. 2. Nuclear arms control--Fiction. 3. Environmental protection--Fiction. 4. Animals and civilization--Fiction. 4. Ecofiction. 5. Fantasy fiction. I. Title.

PS3612.E99 R48 2010

813/.6 2010931184

PRINTED IN THE UNITED STATES OF AMERICA
on acid∞free paper

17 16 15 14 13 12 11 10 01 02 03 04 05 06 07 08

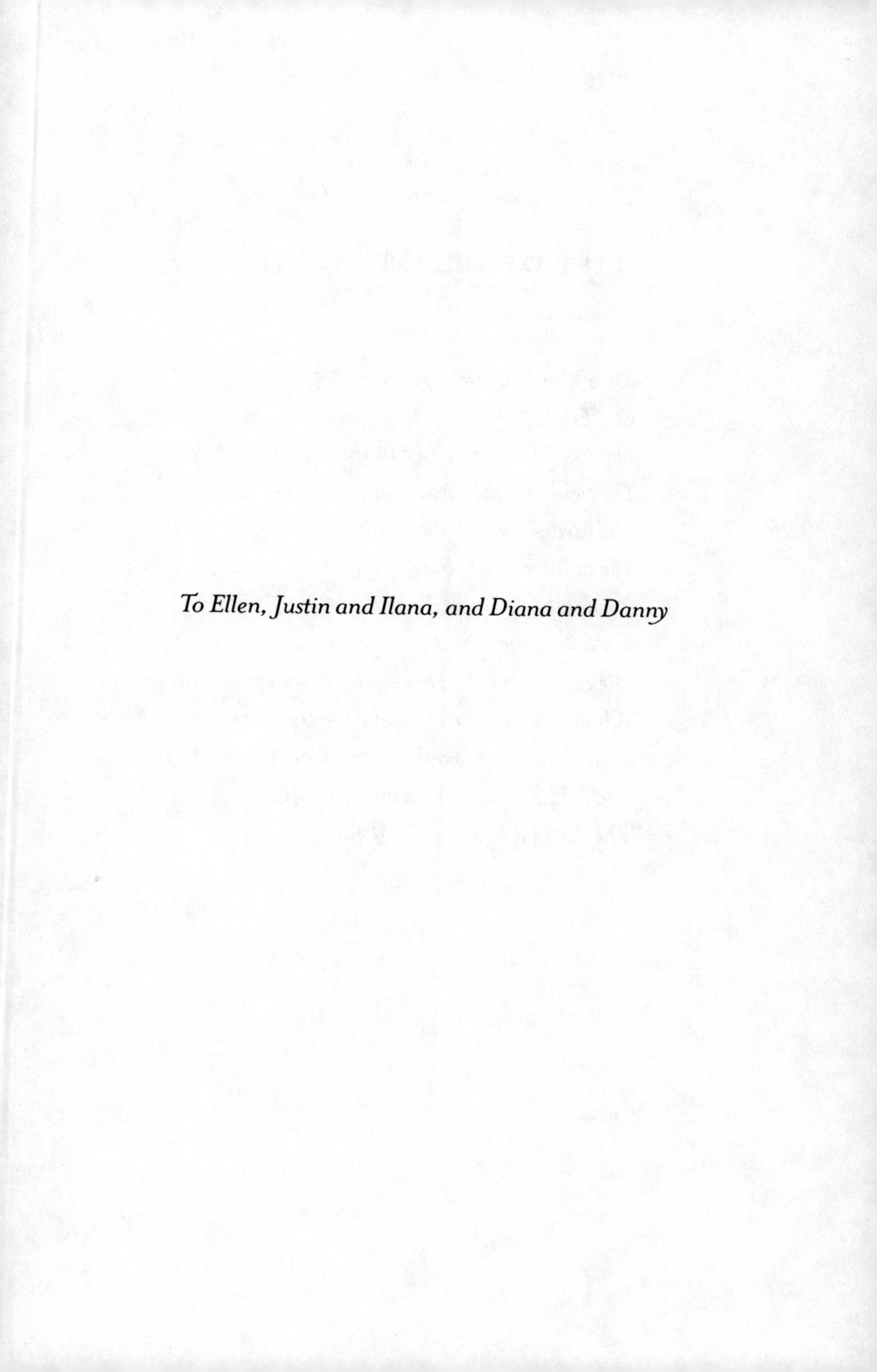

To Ellen, Justin and Ilana, and Diana and Danny

LIST OF ILLUSTRATIONS

Kazen, the Kazakistani rook... 4
Old Eddie flapped his huge ears. 11
The first of the massive cats sprang forward. 28
The field general turtles consult... 45
The turtles develop their battle plans. 52
The vultures take counsel in their eyries... 58
A rat steps over a keyboard... 75
Oola sang the next stanza... 91
The cables absorbed the electrical shocks... 112
"A hole — a puncture!" came the cry. 119
A third vulture looked over the score debris. 126
Old Eddie looked at his mate... 136
"They're at it again!..." 152

TABLE OF CONTENTS

Indian Legend xiii

The Plot 1
The Lady Elephant's Answer 9
Congress Meets 17
The Turtles Move 43
The Generals 51
To Skin a Cat 57
Chernobyl & the Lie 63
The Sea Party 81
The Rays Charge 101
Nibble Fish 109
The Buzzards' Scorecard 123
Delphic Rams Predict Disaster 133
The Viruses & Bacteria 149
Epilogue 161

About the Author 165
About the Illustrator 169
Acknowledgments 171
Colophon 174

Once upon a time, in the beginning days of life upon the earth, man, animals, and plants lived together in equality and mutual helpfulness. Man was one with his environment in a beautiful balance of nature. The needs of all were met in a world of plenty. Man became quite aggressive, however, in his relationship with the rest of his world and began to care less and less for the rights and privileges of others. Soon the harmony was disrupted. Aggressive man was multiplying so rapidly that the other creatures became alarmed and called a meeting of all insects, birds, fishes, reptiles and four-footed beasts. Their hostility, having been provoked, they joined forces against man and devised many diseases to slow down his encroachment upon earth. The bond between man and the other creatures was broken. Man found that his aggressive behavior had brought

much sickness upon him and made it hard for him to secure the food he needed. Many methods were devised to appease the spirits of the animals that he killed for food. The plant life remained friendly to man, however, and when they heard about the many diseases inflicted upon him, they responded by offering themselves as cures and remedies for his ailments. Each tree, herb, shrub, grass and moss devised a cure for man if only he could discover and use it. Thus man created a situation of struggle and turmoil. To have food and to keep himself healthy, he must consider the hostility of animals and the friendship of plant life. He must carefully and prayerfully secure and prepare his meat and plant food within the difficulties that he himself had created. Through the years the delicate art of securing food and medicines developed among the Indian people.

~From an Ancient Indian legend

Revolt *of the* Animals

(and *Their Secret Plan to Save the Earth*)

The Plot

APRIL 1–3

Kazen, the Kazakistani rook, cocked his head, straining to hear bits of conversation drifting through a crack in a window of a backwater Pakistani conference room. Inside, two high-ranking extremists, the early birds of terrorism, sat talking and drinking illegal vodka, not realizing that avian creatures are the most natural of spies.

Fluffing his glossy black feathers, Kazen wiggled his beak, the closest thing to a smile he could manage. *Stupid humans*, he thought. *Because they can't understand us, they think we can't understand them.* He inched closer and stretched his neck to better hear the conversation.

"Our comrades in Syria have been given an ultimatum," said one of the terrorists, a squat little man who threatened to burst from his dark blue *Shalwar-kameez* tunic and pants. His drinking partner, a tall, almost emaciated man, in a brown European style *sardari* jacket, a submachine gun by his side, simply raised an eyebrow.

"They must agree within thirty days to join us in an attack on Israel, or we will blow up Damascus," said the fat one. "And blame the Israelis."

"Clever."

"Yes. And we have nuclear bomb parts smuggled from Israel. Allah be praised."

"Clever, again."

His initial purpose for flying to Peshawar forgotten – to find out if the grain harvest was going to be good – Kazen leaned closer to the window crack.

"Behter," the thin one said, nodding his head forward and down to signify assent. "But how do you propose to keep this scheme from our leader?"

"He is too busy enforcing bans against lipstick, Western attire, and loud music. These efforts provide him distraction to say he does not know our brothers are threatening Syria."

"But you know the Americans will threaten to retaliate against us all," the thin one said, downing the glass of bootleg vodka officials had been unsuccessful in banning, despite the threat of seventy-four lashes, a hefty fine, and three months to a year in prison for violations.

Kazen pecked at imaginary birdseed to conceal his interest, careful to avoid the electronic sensor wires lining the windowsill.

"What will the Americans do, bomb Pakistan AND Syria? Impossible!"

"If they do," said the thin one, grimacing, "better to lose a few of our own people than to allow Israel to control the world." He was clearly worried. "And the British and the French?"

"*Koi masla neih,*" the fat man shook his head. "What will they do but make their usual loud noises about terrorism?"

"And our leader?"

Mr. Squat smiled – a smile that made Kazen's feathers stand on end. "When victory is an accomplished fact, what can he do but claim it was his idea all along? We will let him take the credit, then his health will decline and he will retire." The smile disappeared. The saber by his side rattled.

These humans mean business, thought Kazen. *Don't the jerks realize the United States would be forced to nuke a Middle East target if they followed their plan? Don't they know the result can be total war and the annihilation of every living thing in the world!*

Unable to listen any longer, the rook let out a loud squawk and soared into the sky as dark and cloudy as the terrible news he must spread far and wide. The terrorists are going to stage an attack on Syria as an excuse to destroy Israel.

Kazen, the Kazakistani rook, cocked his head, straining to hear bits of conversation from inside the conference room.

The news of the threat of an extremist-inspired nuclear war spread rapidly throughout the Animal Kingdom, and fears were reinforced by a test blast in India that resulted in the deaths of thousands of large and small animals, fish, and insects. Those not destroyed by the blast died from radiation in the following days and weeks.

The word spread. Nuclear war is not just a theory; it is a reality. And it could set off a chain reaction.

The fox's fur nearly fell from his hide. The mink almost turned from rich brown to white. The polar bear awoke from its winter slumber, angry and hungry.

At first, not everyone in the Animal Kingdom believed the news. The sharks, survivors since the age of dinosaurs, had trouble comprehending the possibility of the end of the world. Creatures with relatively young histories couldn't believe they might not be given a chance to live and grow. The lions, whose pride was great, refused to accept their mortality. Surely the news did not apply to them. The cockroaches simply didn't care. An atomic catastrophe couldn't kill them. Hadn't they survived every disaster known to man – and many before man?

But Kazen and his messengers shouted: You fools! The entire planet is going to be destroyed! Nothing – not a single thing – will survive the final blowup.

Now, even the cockroaches were shaken. The specter of

a thousand million blinding suns exploding at once on the planet they had called home for millenniums was too frightening to be believed, but too horrible to be ignored.

The animals could no longer forget the memory of the birds and fishes that had died eating sprayed and poisoned plants, or from the stench of polluted waters. They couldn't close their eyes to the darkness blotting out the sun, forget the bitter-tasting rain, or overlook the strange color of their streams and estuaries.

The alarm sounded as reports of danger on a scale unimaginable and unheard of in past ages mounted.

We must call another Congress of the insects, birds, fishes, reptiles, and four-footed beasts. We must try to save our earth, they decided.

But how would they set up such a conference? No one alive now had been at the first great Congress of the animals. Millions of species populated the earth. How would they travel the distances to attend such a meeting? Where would it be held? And when? And how could such animals as the fox and the weasel be expected to engage in peaceful dialogue with species such as the rabbit and the chicken? Who would maintain order? Who would feed the multitude? But most of all, how would the creatures go about organizing such an enormous undertaking as saving the world?

A leader must be chosen, someone to take charge. But who?

A poll of the species, with Kazen in charge, determined this leadership should come from the elephants, known for their intelligence and incredible memory. Of all the elephants, only Old Eddie, the ancient pachyderm in the National Zoo in Washington, D.C., had the qualifications. Many non-zoo animals knew of his great understanding and wisdom from their wanderings. He'd settled disputes between various creatures before. Among the animals, great and small, wise and dull, handsome and plain, Old Eddie was the choice.

Of all the creatures, surely Old Eddie would know what to do.

The Lady Elephant's Answer

APRIL 4–6

Old Eddie had no idea what to do. He flapped his huge ears, and shook his five-ton, ten-foot-tall body, shifting his weight from one leaden food to another. Years ago he'd overheard some of the people who gathered outside his bars talking about such places as Hiroshima and Nagasaki, and after hearing what had happened in those cities he had been unable to sleep for days. Why were humans so insensitive to the feelings of animals? Perhaps they didn't realize how much animals understood. How else to explain their discussing death and destruction within earshot?

But not everyone was insensitive. Most people visited the

zoo just to ooh and ahh, and Old Eddie, being a patient animal, didn't mind rearing and waving his reddish-brown trunk in exchange for an occasional peanut toss.

His keepers didn't like for him to have those extra peanuts. They posted signs that read: "Do not feed the animals." To them Old Eddie had just one thing to say: "Braa-cha!" ("Idiots!" in elephant talk.)

But on the whole his keepers were gentle and tolerable. The people he really disliked were those who stood outside the bars muttering about "how easy" the animals had it, while thus and so plagued the world – and then proceeded to discuss the "thus and so." Sometimes he had to resist the urge to spray water on the slouches, but he refrained. Absent clear and present danger, he'd rather turn the other rump.

However, now it seemed the clear and present danger had arrived – if one could believe the reports he'd been receiving from squirrels who crossed the wide moat separating the metal fence from the elephant walks and dropped morsels of information in Old Eddie's ears, or cowbirds or sparrows, who liked the smell of elephant life and carried comments on the wings of birds from as far away as Australia. Other zoo inhabitants with friends on the "outside" quickly relayed information to Old Eddie. As he sifted the data and sniffed the air, all evidence pointed to danger—extreme danger. In a matter of days, if something wasn't done, the terrorists would drop

Old Eddie flapped his huge ears.

their bombs on Israel. When the delegations of birds and creepy crawly things had approached him about a second great Congress, he had not been surprised, only dumbfounded to be asked to *lead* that Congress.

At first, Eddie hesitated. Normally, he liked at least a month or two to make the simplest of decisions, and this one was far from simple. But how could he refuse? Finally, his sense of responsibility overcame his stubborn streak.

Tradition dictated that the second Congress take place where the first Congress had been held—on the great plains of Eastern Europe. But no one knew which plains. And even if they had, the balance of power had shifted. The greatest number of complaints came from species in the United States and Russia. Logic pointed to either Russia or America as the place to hold the meeting, but as Eddie noted, the creatures in Russia weren't receptive to the idea. Not surprising, considering that he'd heard entire flocks of elk and caribou had been slaughtered in pogroms lasting a single night. And informants were everywhere.

That left the United States. But where? The Midwest, although centrally located, was still inconvenient to many creatures. Almost every creature had a different suggestion. The alligators and the crocodiles demanded the meeting be held in the Everglades, but the pelicans, beavers, and woodchucks said, "No way! We're not about to provide the 'gators and the crocs with the meal of their lives!" And of course, the mountain goats insisted on holding the meeting on the slopes of Mt. McKinley, and various fish offered a fine lagoon off Nags Head, North Carolina. Old Eddie's mate complained of droppings in her food from birds flying about.

"Will you please make up your mind," trumpeted Gra'ma Elka, "so I can eat a decent meal?"

"I'm sorry about your food," said Old Eddie, "but I won't be stampeded into a decision."

Gra'ma Elka wasn't the only one pushing him. As he deliberated locations over and over again, the other creatures were becoming concerned. They don't have my patience, thought Old Eddie. He really couldn't blame them. Some had a life span only a fraction of an elephant's. But tradition was tradition. If he was going to change the location of the meeting, he'd better have an excellent reason. No matter what place he chose, vast numbers of creatures would be unable to attend because of distance, topography, food supply, or what have you.

Gra'ma Elka waddled out of the wading pool and stretched out on her side to dry. "Life is good," she said, in the non-human Esperanto that transcends yet links all animals. "For many years, I hated this zoo. But I must admit, they feed us well, nurse us when we're sick, and provide us with food and water. I'd rather be in the wilds, but for a welfare state, this place is not half bad. And I think most of the other animals agree."

Most of the other animals agree. The words stuck in Old Eddie's mind. He swatted his side with his trunk. "Braa-cha!" (Eddie, you idiot!) In a rare display of affection (they mated only a few times a year), he embraced Elka, then reared his massive head, raised his trunk and trumpeted: "*The Congress will be held in the National Zoo at the next full moon!*"

The animals in the nearby cages and compounds jumped at the sound. What was all the commotion?

Again the trumpeting. This time, no one failed to hear. A troop of birds took flight and began spreading the news far and wide—except for one buzzard.

"Are you sure, elder?" asked the buzzard, addressing Old Eddie in a respectful tone. "Should you consider this decision for a day or two?"

"No, I have decided. Now go!" said Old Eddie. "Spread the good news. We meet here at the full moon."

The buzzard took off to notify his fellow carrion-eaters west of the Rockies. *I'll spread the news all right, but it won't be good news to us,* he thought. *We're on the side of the humans. Disasters are our bread and butter. The danger of these upsets ending all life on earth are just wild exaggerations. Oh sure, the population on earth will be reduced, but the buzzards, falcons, vultures, owls, hawks, and eagles will have more food than we've ever dreamed of—a coast-to-coast cafeteria of corpses. No fat, stupid elephant is going to stop that!*

The buzzard pounded his wings furiously. He must hurry to take the news to his friends. Together, they would find a way to foul up this great meeting and help the humans.

Congress Meets

APRIL 10

Four more days passed. A full moon hung over the zoo, the time when lovers supposedly go wild, madness increases, and wolves howl.

Lulled by the mild April weather, visitors to the zoo lingered under the trees, enjoying a cool drink before wandering home. Whether they forgot or were too affected by the general languor, the zoo keepers failed to shoo everyone out until fifteen minutes past the official 8 p.m. closing time. As the last visitor disappeared, Old Eddie sighed with relief. The keepers began making their rounds and soon they too melted into the night.

And not a moment too soon. Tension had been building the past three days as the birds and animals arrived from every corner of the globe, some rarely seen in this part of the world. Night hawks from southern Canada, lesser golden plovers from Alaska and the Hawaiian Islands, Arctic terns from Asia, and birds of paradise and toucans from South America settled on the trees, waiting. The eyes of hundreds of creatures from the farthest reaches of the world glowed from the shrubbery.

Old Eddie had sent the mockingbirds to monitor all approaches to Washington with instructions to spot any creatures by their sounds, then guide them in. The mockers did their job well, but still the mass influx was not without incident. An unusually large number of animals were struck by motorists. Others, being distant from their habitats, collapsed in exhaustion, hunger, and thirst. Still others, despite their finely-honed instincts, traveled in circles. So many rabbits, unable to return to their homes, settled with other rabbits in a Howard County, Maryland, farming community that it came to resemble Easter year-round. And so many transplanted foxes bivouacked in Fauquier County, Virginia, the hounds of the local fox-hunters quickly exhausted themselves giving chase.

Still, most delegates arrived safely. Some settled in the grass and bushes bordering nearby Rock Creek Park. Resident park animals grumbled at having to share space and food with such a horde, but Old Eddie's emissaries assured them the inconvenience would be brief. Old Eddie hoped the meeting could be concluded after one night. For days, each species in the zoo had hidden a portion of their rations to share with the creatures most closely aligned with them. Visiting monkeys dined with the zoo's lesser apes; crows with macaws; and the pigs, who disliked traveling any farther than the barn to the trough, dined with their long-snouted cousins, the peccaries. Other creatures, including groundlings and birds, foraged their food, some flying as far as the Chesapeake Bay to dine.

As the moon moved higher in the sky, the delegates, in compatible animal groups, hovered in bushes, trees, and grass near the elephant walk, swapping stories of their adventures en route to the Congress. A terrifying trumpeting sound from Old Eddie brought about immediate and total silence.

"Welcome, one and all," roared Old Eddie, his large black eyes sweeping the crowded walkways, benches, trees, hillsides, and mounds. Eyes of all shapes, sizes, and colors looked back at him, reflected by light from the many lampposts.

"According to my calculations," began Old Eddie, "in twenty days the terrorists will drop nuclear bombs on Syria. But many of you claim the greater threat is from environmental destruction. Still others raise petty concerns. We must share information and decide what to do. We can only deal with the important problems. So I ask, what's more important? The environment, the terrible weapons, or some other matter?"

Hoots, howls, cries, and grunts followed as every creature began talking at once from their sections along the elephant walk. The porcupines, who Old Eddie assigned to maintain order, patrolled constantly, urging calm. The mockers announced which kind of creature was to speak, and in what order. Each group had elected a leader. A hawk raised his large grey wings and was recognized.

"The farmers no longer let their chickens run free. They coop them up where they're harder to snatch," said the hawk. "When we do occasionally catch one, it doesn't taste like it did in the old days."

"That's because the chickens never see the sun, nor eat the fresh grasses of the barnyard," said Old Eddie. "They eat a rigid, controlled diet, so every processed chicken will be the same size and color. I've heard some farmers put cement in the chickens' diets to make the shells harder."

"Disgusting," said the hawk, beady eyes wide with fright.

"You should hear what the chickens think about it," said Old Eddie. "It's bad enough to be bred solely for market, but most never even see the sun before they die."

Two chickens and a rooster, who had escaped from a farm thirty miles away, hung their heads. "This is the first time we've eaten wild seeds," they said, pointing to the fallout from nearby beech and pine trees, "and we will never return to that farm."

"You'll freeze in the winter," said a practical squirrel.

"We should live so long," said the rooster, shaking his comb. Seeing his proud gestures, a fair number of creatures cheered, especially when he drew the chickens under his wings.

When the noise subsided, a beautiful white angora spoke on behalf of the lesser cats. "What's all the hubbub about?" she purred. "Sure, there are fewer table scraps than there used to be, but we cats aren't suffering. The planet dying? We don't see it."

The other animals, especially the dogs, cried out, accusing the cats of being insulated from the world's problems—uncaring, insensitive. "What do you dogs know?" whined a manx, "You're so stupid you chase cars and get killed. Who's going to listen to you?"

Two large greyhounds bolted over the dividing hillside. Had not two porcupines named Quiller and Stickrod jumped in front of the cats, the hounds would have had them by the throat. Other creatures, as much for their own safety as for the cats, cried out in every tongue for peace.

"What kind of an example are we for the humans, if we can't keep peace among ourselves?" asked a sensible old mare, her hoarse voice cutting through the hubbub. All action stopped.

"Now aren't you ashamed of yourselves?" chided Old Eddie. "There will be no more disturbances, or I will immediately adjourn the Congress and send everyone packing."

At that moment, the buzzards, who had been biding their time, swooped down on a sleeping mouse, not to eat him, but to cause pandemonium. Mice, rats, and other rodents dashed about, shrieking. The meeting might well have ended had not a lion let out a roar so enormous it sent a shiver down the spine of every creature within earshot. No matter that the great cat was caged. His mighty roar sounded as though he could pierce steel.

The buzzards flew back to their roosts; the rodents returned to their places. The great cat had once more proven he indeed was King of the Beasts.

"I still don't see why we should help the humans," hissed a copperhead as everyone settled down. "They destroy our breeding grounds, and capture and kill us. They turn us into handbags and shoes, and never give us a moment's peace. Why help them?"

"Who said anything about helping humans?" growled a wolf. "I have as many complaints as you. They shoot and poison us. Take our furs and sell them. They track our spoor and trap us. They describe bad people, like sex maniacs, or someone who kills for the fun of it, as 'wolves in sheep's clothing.' As though wolves ever did such things. I have no love for humans, my hatred runs deep." The wolf bared his teeth, causing the neighboring animals to shrink back. "I say it's time to inflict new diseases on man, as our forefathers did."

"Hear, hear," clapped a grey pigeon on a high branch, causing a dropping to fall on the wolf's paw. The wolf wiped it off in disgust. The pigeon covered her face with her wings, then flew away.

"I'm not happy about some of my fine feathered friends, either," growled the wolf, frowning at the fleeing pigeon, "but every creature that flies, walks, or crawls on the earth has a right to life, liberty, and the pursuit of happiness. Is that not true, brother elephant? Is that not what our ancestors decreed at the first great Congress?"

"That is what my father, and his father before him, passed on to me—yes," said Old Eddie.

Gra'ma Elka nodded. Two younger elephants, less sure of what happened at the great meeting, but who believed Eddie and Elka, also voiced agreement. "The trouble is," said the one named Rachel, "old diseases caused after the first Congress just gave us a breathing space, but in the long run, what did they accomplish? People are killing at newfound speed, except perhaps in India, where vegetarianism and respect for the cow is deeply ingrained. Imagine people eating animal blood and calling it gravy! What if we ate *their* blood and called it soup?"

A great outpouring followed.

One woodchuck became sick. The other young elephant, Uriah, not wanting the session sidetracked, shouted over the noise, "The state of man's science is so advanced that any new diseases might be isolated and cured in ten or fifty years.

Ailments are no longer the answer. We must neutralize man's enormous destructive capability."

"Dam up the rivers of the world," shouted a beaver through protruding teeth. "That'll cause a heck of a lot of problems."

"Oh, yeah," chirped a yellow-eyed vireo, "that might work—if we had fifty million beavers for every dam, instead of one beaver for every fifty million dams."

"What could we possibly do to make the humans save the world?" asked an innocent young colt, addressing the wolf.

The wolf thought for a moment. "No," he said, "we can't make humans save the world. What we must do, brothers, is make it impossible for them to *destroy* the world. We must confound them, confuse them, bewilder them—destroy their will, and their means to harm us."

"A tall, tall order if I ever heard one," snorted a pig. "Nullify man's capacity to destroy the world? You might as well get a cow to birth a sheep, or a bull to adopt a piglet."

"Or a fox to feed a bear. Or a chimp to raise a hamster," said another pig.

"Or an eagle to raise a snake, or a—"

"Enough, enough," said a guinea hen. "What are you getting at?"

"What I am getting at," said one of the pigs, "is that to hamper the dirty humans, we'll have to have contact with them. And we've had more than enough contact already. If I hear 'bring home the bacon,' 'you stupid pig,' ' don't make a pig of yourself,' or 'stop pigging out,' one more time, I'll scream."

"Stop repeating yourselves," said a goose, flapping her wings. "Say what you mean."

"Braa-cha!" trumpeted Old Eddie.

"See? See?" shrieked the pigs. They knew Old Eddie's word for idiots. "Now even the animals are criticizing us!"

"Well, we don't have all night," bleated a goat.

"I thought we did," said the second pig.

"For discussion. Not for pigs."

"That comment was unnecessary," chorused the pigs, drawing close. "Besides, we'll never get organized enough to hurt the humans. What we want is agreement that we'll have no contact with them in any way," they said looking about. "Let's take to the hills, and when the days of torment and nights of killing are no more, we'll return and take over."

"If there's still a planet left to take over," honked a gray goose. "Just the kind of greedy suggestion I'd expect from a pig!"

"Here, here!" cooed the formerly embarrassed pigeon, now returned, but perched on a tree far from the wolf.

The pigeon's remark wasn't understood. The pig's suggestion was quickly passed over. No one wanted to take to the hills. As one muskrat said, disagreeing with the oinkers, "Who's going to feed such a mammoth population if we take to the hills? What hills have sufficient food and water, not to say housing for millions of animals? And the trails would be so jammed that most of the animals would die long before they reached the hills."

Most of the delegates nodded their approval. But the vultures, brothers to the buzzards, refused to let the opportunity pass. "The Rocky Mountains," they cried. "Hills aplenty! Hills and dales! Valleys and peaks! Thousands of unspoiled acres! Plenty of room, for every animal and fish and flying bird. Many of us live there, and so can you! Plenty of underground caverns, too, where you can burrow until the planet becomes habitable again."

"And what will you be doing, Mr. Real Estate Salesman, while we're in hiding?" squawked a sea gull.

"Why, we'll be your scouts—let you know when the land and air are safe again."

"I bet," sniffed the sea gull. "No one will ever be safe from you carrion-eaters."

The moon moved behind a cloud bank, plunging the convocation into darkness. A cry rang out, followed by a moan. The moon reappeared, revealing the owls as they lifted several rodents into the air. Every small animal within fifty feet scattered, trampling other animals in their path. The dogs interpreted this as open season on the cats and began tearing after the felines.

The pigs squealed with delight. The vultures nodded

approvingly, swooping down to pick up the entrails of any mowed-down animals.

Then Old Eddie trumpeted a signal.

A dozen raccoons and woodchucks quickly assembled on a mound beyond the tiger cage. A second signal from Old Eddie, and they tore against the mound with their sharp teeth, destroying the last barrier to a forty-foot tunnel they'd built the past few nights. At the same moment, the tigers lunged through the tunnel from the other end. A few moments and the first of the massive cats sprang forth, followed quickly by the other three. Each tiger was responsible for a quadrant of the park. With one bold stroke, tiger number one, assigned to the northern field, tore out the throat of a falcon feeding on several field mice. Other birds of prey scattered to the upper branches of an elm. One dropped a mouse from his mouth and it fell to the ground. The great cat carefully lifted him on its paw and sat him down on a small tuft of grass where other mice cowered.

Another tiger stomped on an owl picking at the intestines of a squawking chicken, demolishing them both. Two dogs cornered a pregnant Cheshire cat and tossed her about, leaving behind only the feline's smile.

Although most of the birds behaved, a few took advantage of the confusion to hunt the many earthworms, but they were sent flying by a fourth tiger's angry approach. A pig who had

The first of the massive cats sprang forward.

kicked at a quail's eggs was sent squealing to its pile of dirt. The pig tried to camouflage itself by rolling in mud, but the tiger, uninterested in further pursuit, roared off after several mountain goats who had locked horns with a ram.

"Stop! Stop!" trumpeted Old Eddie.

Total silence.

The tigers ceased roaring; the various animals stopped dead in their tracks. Although the fight was over, many animals looked warily about. Would the tigers make short order of them also? But Old Eddie had foreseen that possibility. He'd made sure the tigers had plenty to eat the past few days by arranging to have various birds find extra food and carry it to them. Not that tigers were underfed by the keepers, but better they be stuffed silly, than merely adequately fed before their first whiff of freedom among such a diversified crowd. But the tigers didn't crawl back into their holes. As Old Eddie had directed, they fanned out, each taking up a position of sixty yards apart to guard against further disorder.

As the various animals regrouped and licked their wounds, ever more cautious, an old zebra asked Eddie to recommend a course of action while there were still enough animals alive to vote.

"Well stated," said Old Eddie, heart heavy and eyes misty, blaming himself for the turmoil. True, he'd foreseen the possibilities, but had hoped the worst would not happen. And now it had. And at what price?

Old Eddie glanced at the moon, now three-quarters across the heavens. Something must be done here and now before dawn. Clearly, this meeting would not last a second night. Democracy was fine, but it must not be allowed to degenerate into anarchy. Rights must be tempered with responsibility. He hadn't wanted to forcibly terminate the discussion. He preferred a full airing of views with every creature in agreement, especially on the life and death issue facing them, but now he realized this consensus was his dream. He couldn't impose his goal on everyone, no matter how attractive. Unanimity was out; majority vote was in. Could he hope even for that?

An elephant is nothing if not determined. Eddie heaved his massive body this way and that and lumbered to the center of the elephant walk. He waited a moment for the hubbub to subside.

"We must decide—and now—whether to turn our backs on impending destruction, and hope for the best, or," he said with newfound force and urgency, "decide tonight to move forward. Commit ourselves this moment! Do all of us believe we must act now to save the planet? All those in favor of stopping the war machine, speak up."

A loud wave of whistles, woofs, waving of various appendages, and general cheering greeted his words.

Now came the hard part. "How many do not agree?" he almost whispered.

The birds of prey screeched. The pigs grunted. But their sounds were but a fraction of those who cheered.

"All right, then it's clear we want action," said Old Eddie, moving quickly to the next topic before the larger issue could be noticed and questioned. Some creatures decided to follow the wishes of others. No stampede or fire pushed them into one direction or another. Bears voted with birds. Sheep paired with tigers, and even the out-voted pigs and buzzards, despite their misgivings, apparently accepted the will of the majority. Old Eddie knew history of a sort was being made, but he dare not draw attention to it.

"Next question: What is our priority? Do we stop the humans from poisoning our water and food, or do we stop them from producing weapons of war?" asked Old Eddie, deciding not to raise a third or fourth possibility lest someone demand it; the fewer choices, the quicker the Congress would end. He'd thought long and hard. He knew what the choice had to be anyway, if anything *could* be done.

"All those in favor of stopping the war machine, speak up."

A tumult, louder than the cries of approval to the first

question followed. No one noticed that a majority of creatures were telling the minority what to do.

"All those who wish to focus on the food and water supplies, speak up!"

Again, many cries. Almost as many as had cheered in favor of stopping the war machine. Many delegates, though moved by the specter of extinction, found the issue of annihilation abstract, while the daily search for decent food and water seemed practical. How they would be able to find worthwhile food and water on a planet ravaged by nuclear war they could not explain. Old Eddie understood why many delegates had voted in favor of both competing resolutions. Nevertheless, the resolution to stop the war machine had won. He announced this to more cheers, but with more than a few boos and hisses from the dissenters.

Now that the goal had been decided, the meeting broke out into all sorts of wrangling about how to achieve it.

A black bear from the far side of the zoo sent word that everyone should go on a hunger strike.

"Fine for a bear, who hibernates all winter," piped a robin, "but what am I to tell my brood? They need to be fed nineteen times a day."

"Yes, why make the little children suffer?" cried a skunk. "My offspring never stop eating. And even if every skunk in creation keeled over, would that convince the humans to live different lives?"

The hunger strike suggestion might have died at that point, had not an orangutan leaping from tree to tree suggested that a hunger strike might work for pet dogs and cats because surely their loving masters would notice and respond to it.

A wail of protest rose from the cats and dogs. A chocolate-colored dachshund, known more for his articulateness than his size, argued, "Why should *we* be asked to sacrifice for everyone else? Besides, I like my three squares as well as anyone else."

"You eat three times a day?" asked a tabby.

"I have an indulgent master. When he eats, I eat. He's probably running around right now, waving the supper dish, crying, 'Here Scout. Here Scout.'"

A few creatures laughed, but most looked at him critically. It was clear that combating the overwhelming power of the humans wasn't going to be easy. Sacrifices that would contribute to the success of the fight must be accepted with grace and good feeling, if not for one's own sake, then for the sake of future generations. Sensing this, the dachshund said, "If a hunger strike by the dogs and cats is what it takes, I'll not only participate, I'll lead the way."

With impeccable logic Old Eddie nixed the suggestion. "Some creatures will no doubt die in the struggle against the humans," he said. "But there's no point in uselessly seeking death. Not one human in a million will understand what is going on. They'll think some mysterious disease is claiming their pets. And if by some magic they do understand that animals aren't eating as a form of protest, they won't understand why. And even if they're told why, they'll never believe it. No. A hunger strike will merely produce martyrs and not further our goal."

Overwhelmed, the dachshund shrank away, tail between his legs.

"Eat all the humans," suggested the lion. "Then let's see them make war."

From the raccoons: "Ransack their garbage. Make a mess of their cities."

To which an urban pigeon replied: "Obviously, these raccoons have never seen New York City!"

A gray squirrel: "Why not create havoc on every farm in Russia and America? Withhold their food supply!"

To which the chickens clucked and a cow mooed: "Impossible! Might as well ask a squirrel to grow fins or a bear to fly—"

"Or a horse to adopt a toad," shouted a pig, hoping this time no one would shut him up. No one did. They were all too busy worrying about losing the qualities that made them animals, not rocks or humans.

"Some things we cannot do," said the rooster, draping his wings about his nervous brood.

Gra'ma Elka had watched everything with growing dismay. She edged her mate aside. "I can see the first streaks of orange over the far hills," she said. "Dawn will soon be here. Propose something sensible. There must be something we can do that will work."

If there was, no one could think of it. For the first time that night everyone seemed tongue-tied. They glanced at each other critically for not being able to offer helpful suggestions. Even the birds were quiet. A wave of hopelessness flowed through the crowd, drawn faces and wide eyes reflecting sagging hopes. Had not a creature no one ever expected to hear from found his voice, the Congress might have collapsed at that moment.

"Nobody can make a war if it isn't properly documented," said a small turtle, with a deep, booming voice that sounded like he lived in a box.

A sea of perplexed eyes turned to the turtle.

"It's quite simple," said the turtle, stretching as far outside his shell as possible. "We've all heard humans talk about the Holocaust. Millions of Jews were killed, but they were nothing compared to the billions of flying insects and animals trampled, bombed, burned, sprayed, and buried alive during the great war. Humans don't count us among the casualties because—" he cleared his throat. "But I digress," he said, taking a sip from a nearby mud puddle, "and my voice won't hold out. Let me get to the point."

"Please do," said Gra'ma Elka, one eye on the first rays of light illuminating the blue tail feathers of a condor high in a sycamore.

"Well, well," said the turtle, dark eyes shining, "I once heard some hunters say that because the Nazis destroyed all the papers relating to the Holocaust, no proof existed that it had ever occurred. I know those hunters were stupid because the Nazis kept their paperwork, and many animals know about those death camps, and I also know that destroying the paperwork can't undo an event, but perhaps it can prevent an event from happening!"

The other animals stared at each other, confused. But as no one had a better suggestion the turtle was allowed to continue.

"Don't you see?" stammered the turtle, "If we destroy all the files relating to the next war, the humans can't fight. Without their paperwork, there's no way the superpowers can move their armies, or fire their missiles! Wreck their paperwork, foul up their computers, and they're finished!"

"Destroy paperwork?"

"Ruin machines?"

"What's he talking about?"

"How could we do that?"

"Easy," said the turtle. "It's so simple, it's hard to see. We have the perfect helpers!" He cranked his neck before delivering his *piece de resistance*. "Our friends, the mice."

"Our friends?"

"Whose friends?"

"What?"

"Who?"

And finally, from the lightning bug, in a voice so tiny it made the turtle sound like a *basso profundo*, "Is he for real?"

The message was passed upward.

"Why are they picking on us?" asked the mice, realizing they now were the center of attention.

"I'm not picking on you," said the turtle, "and I am for real. I listen. I hear. We've all heard. The humans are always complaining about drowning in paperwork. Photocopying machines are to society what printing presses were 150 years ago. Today everyone's his own publisher. If you want to get anything done, you must make fifty copies and send one to everybody. Beeps and blips on computers are starting to replace mounds of paper, but still the push is on putting everything in writing—especially complex technical matters. A hundred different committees must study them before approval. Why, there are probably a thousand sheets of paper just describing where a nuclear missile is housed in a Class B submarine. Multiply that by the millions of papers floating around every day. The possibilities are staggering."

After a quick conference, the mice, now the objects of all the attention, said, "We don't like the sound of it. It exposes us to too much danger. Why, a couple of poisoned holes and we'd all be dead. The argument doesn't hold."

Old Eddie raised his trunk to the side of his head, thinking. The trunk came down. Thought completed. "No, the argument does hold, because in this case there's a worthwhile goal connected to your efforts. That is, the turtle is right. The humans' war machine would be stymied."

"And for the first time in history," said another turtle, who in a world ruled by animals might have become its top ambassador, "mice would be heroes. Think of that—heroic mice, or mice heroes."

The mice beamed and puffed out their chests.

"Why, mice could shred every document of war in half a day, with time out for lunch," declared another turtle.

"Those documents *will* be lunch!" the head mouse exploded.

If that remark was meant as a joke, no one laughed. If it meant an implicit acceptance of the assignment, and it was, it produced a curious reaction, one of respectful silence, as if everyone understood a line had been crossed. Talk was over. The time for action had begun. Someone had volunteered—or had been dragooned into accepting—a dangerous task! Accompanying the silence was an element of fear and even dread. Who would be next? What other group would have to volunteer? Who would die?

Clearly all hopes could not be pinned on the lowly mice and their confederates. What if they failed? Or, conversely, succeeded, but their efforts were not sufficient? The cooperation of other animals, including the larger and stronger ones, would be needed. Would not back-up plans be necessary?

Yes, they all agreed. And the excellent suggestions of the turtles generated considerable follow-up planning. In the time left before the dawn broke completely (and, in truth, the meeting did not adjourn until one minute before the zoo opened at 6 a.m.) the animals made tremendous progress. By the time the park gates clanged open, the creatures had planned no fewer than nine attacks to be launched simultaneously with that of the mice. If one attack failed, the others would succeed. If even more failed, one or two would certainly work.

In the process of deciding the courses of action, Old Eddie resolved a problem of great concern to him—who would be his field generals. The animals on the front lines must be those not penned in the zoo, and those who had sufficient intelligence, mobility, and good sense to lead this worthy war on the humans. Yes, the question of who would coordinate the attacks had answered itself at the right moment, like so many things in life. Although the turtles lacked speed, they did have the mobility and other leadership qualities. They would be the field generals! They would lead the way!

The Turtles Move

APRIL 11

The turtles wished they lived someplace else. Like Africa, where they could hide, or Asia where they were revered and respected by the traditional Asians who saw them as four-legged counterparts to old people—wise and thoughtful, and worthy of respect because they'd experienced and suffered so much. Not like in America where the typical turtle met his maker by being run over by a car, or, worse yet, wound up in turtle soup.

It was something of a surprise to the turtles that Joshua, one of their own, had been listened to at the Congress, and had been nominated to be—what was it Old Eddie had said? —field generals. This was overwhelming. Field generals of what? Of all the other animals? The idea that tigers, lions, and bears would take orders from turtles was preposterous. And even if the other animals did listen to them, what would they say? And do?

While the turtles conferred, the zoo keepers cleaned up from what appeared to have been an invasion of marauding vandals the previous night. Trash cans had been overturned and food scraps dropped willy-nilly. Grassy hills and dales had been reduced to muddy plats. Also, the marauders seemed to have brought a bunch of wild animals with them, for the footprints of four-legged creatures were everywhere. Thankfully, the hoodlums hadn't harmed any of the caged animals. But another incursion of this sort must be prevented. Who knows what might happen next time? Guards manned the gates and patrolled the zoo the following night.

However, the hired sentinels didn't see a group of six turtles who waded out of the seals' pool and made their way over several hills, past a trash can and a water fountain, across a sidewalk, and to the bars of the elephant area. There, they slid down a wall, crossed a moat, and climbed the far wall, reaching Old Eddie's compound three hours later.

Eddie graciously offered the turtles a bite to eat, but unfortunately he had only hay and grass. His guests politely declined, then began to talk.

"We just don't believe we're suited for leadership of mighty

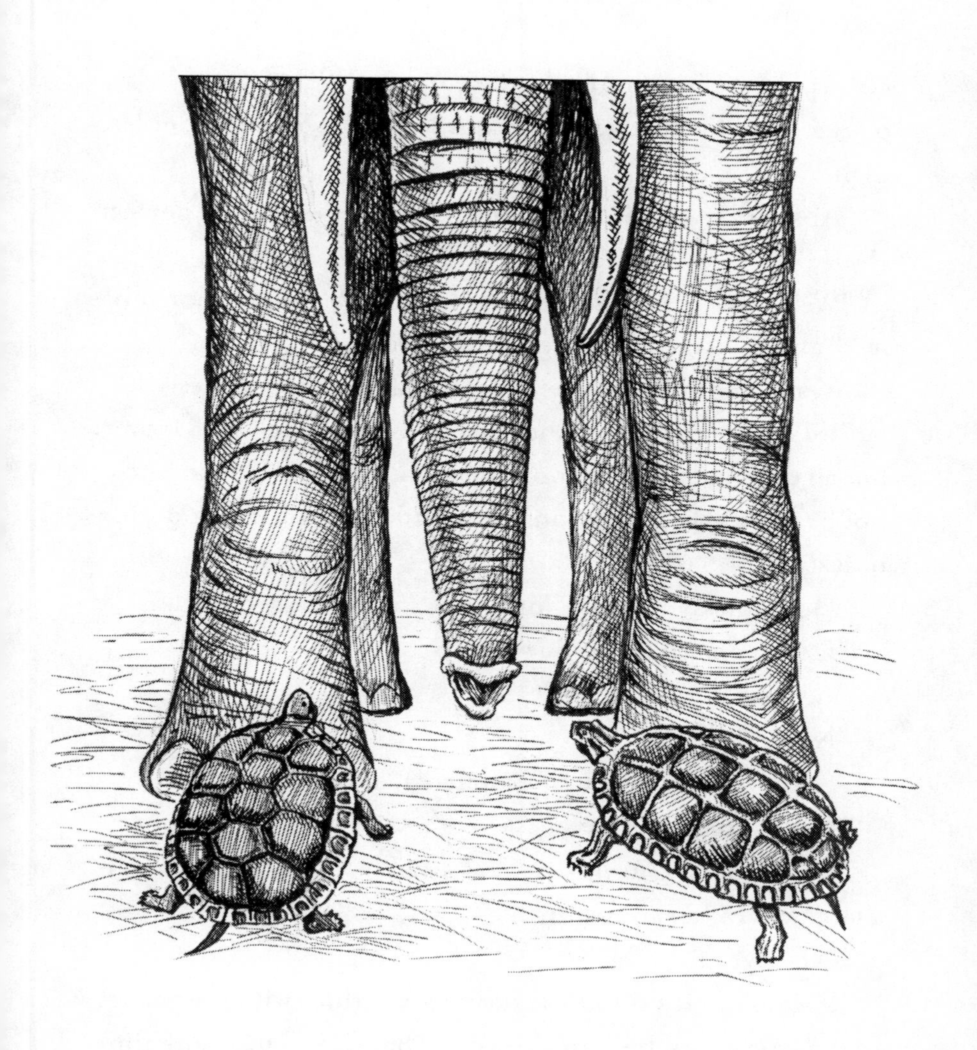

The field general turtles consult with Old Eddie.

enterprises," began one of the turtles. "We'd like to be replaced—say, by the tigers, who did so well restoring order last night!"

"Absolutely not," said Eddie. "You turtles are the perfect choice!"

"Well, can we have some time to consider the responsibility?" another turtle hemmed and hawed.

"Yes, we need more time," chorused the other turtles.

"I'd like to give you all the time in the world to think it over, but all the time might be no time at all, considering there may not be any world before long," said Eddie. "You'd best decide quickly."

"How quickly?" asked Cornelius, a middle-aged turtle.

"How much time do you want?"

"A...year?"

"Never."

"Six months?" ventured Calpurnia, a young female.

"Impossible."

"Thirty days? Surely that's reasonable," offered Vespasian, a large but rather young turtle.

"No way."

It wasn't as if Old Eddie didn't empathize with the turtles. In their position, he probably would have asked for more time to think, too. He'd taken his time calling for the Congress, but now that the meeting had been held, he must seize on the enthusiasm and momentum. To delay even a short time might be fatal.

Sensing this uncommon urgency in Old Eddie, a creature who, like them, was known for his slow, measured gait and unhurried nature, the turtles asked, "When do you need a decision?"

"By tomorrow night," said Eddie.

"Impossible! Never!" shouted three of the turtles; the others merely stared at each other in disbelief.

But there was little more to say. So they inched their way back to the seal pool, via the wall, the moat, and the trash can. "That windbag Joshua got us into this," complained Calpurnia. "He thinks he's a big enough talker to mate every female in creation. Now he's compromised us all!"

"I told him to lay low and shut up," said Ethan, a comrade who until now had been silent. "But no, he had to open his big mouth."

"But he did speak rather well, didn't he?" murmured Florence, who had once mated with Joshua, and was now much sought after by the widowed Cornelius, whose mate had been decapitated by a lawnmower.

"Spoke well? What do you mean by that?" Cornelius harrumphed.

"Now, don't get testy," gurgled Florence, rubbing her neck gently against Cornelius's. "I just meant we've been sticking our heads into our shells more than usual of late. How long can we continue to do this? Joshua made me think yesterday. He made me realize that not facing problems is wrong. We have a moral obligation—yes—an obligation to face our responsibility—and now!"

Calpurnia almost toppled off a log she was crossing, but the others, sobered by the events of the past days and Eddie's urgings, assented one by one. By the time they reached the pool, they had little difficulty in convincing the more than forty other turtles in the larger group to do what Florence had suggested, especially with Joshua's enthusiastic backing. They even bowed to the inevitable and named Joshua as their leader.

The pigeons immediately relayed the other turtles' decision to Old Eddie. The following dawn, he summoned certain sea gulls and they transported the turtles, including one newborn, to a small pond on a deserted island near the headwaters of the Potomac River. There, they would plan their strategy in safety and seclusion with an abundance of natural food and water.

The Generals

APRIL 12

After a hearty breakfast of insects, the turtles gathered the next morning to discuss battle strategy.

Joshua began by asking: "What is a leader? What exactly does a leader do?" Then answering his own question: "A good leader is hard on the outside, but compassionate on the inside. Without ability to inspire, he cannot lead. And without sensitivity, he does not deserve to succeed. A strong leader knows his assignment backwards and forwards, inside and out. Now, I ask you, who is better equipped to be a leader than a turtle?"

The other turtles looked at each other. "What office is he running for?" whispered someone.

The turtles develop their battle plans.

"Who's better equipped to be a leader than a turtle?" repeated Joshua, his wrinkled head bobbing and weaving. Then getting down to business: "Surprise is important in winning battles, but advance planning counts for more. We must review our plans carefully." He beckoned the turtle-generals to come closer.

Some of the plans proposed at the Congress were scrapped; some accepted as is; others refined with subtle improvements. One entirely new plan was adopted. And one or two adult turtles were assigned to each operation. Their instructions: learn everything from aardvarks to zebras about each plan, with special emphasis on the habitats, needs, and traits of the animals, birds, insects, or four-footed beasts upon whom they would have to rely to carry out each plan.

"I once lived with Florence near a place called Fort Meade," said Titus, "and I used to hear the soldiers say, 'If anything can get screwed up, it will.' Applied to our situation, we must all learn what is likely to go awry. And then we must figure out how to make it go right. Study every phase of an attack. What's to be done by whom, in what number and order. And with what result. And have a back-up plan in case of failure. Examine all problem areas. Finally, determine all points of entry, exit, and escape. Creatures will more likely follow you if they know you've planned a safe retreat..."

And so on and on the talk went hour after hour. The gulls,

who knew every creature that walked, swam, or flew, shared their knowledge. Soon the turtle-generals knew almost as much as the gulls. Much would have to be left to chance and to the discretion of whatever creatures would be engaged in a particular operation, of course; but what could be planned in advance was planned well.

Or so they hoped.

To Skin a Cat

APRIL 13

Having originated the phrase "There's more than one way to skin a cat" long before humans "discovered" it, the buzzards, hawks, kites, vultures, and other birds of prey were only briefly set back by their failure to thwart the will of the meeting of the animals.

They took counsel in their eyries in the Rockies to do their own planning. With the attempted disruption of the humans' war machine might come some miscalculations, but, indeed, miscalculations should be encouraged. Given a gentle shove by the birds of prey, might not the best-laid plans of mice

The vultures take counsel in their eyries in the Rockies
to do their own planning.

and turtles go astray? And might not war be the unintended result?

How glorious! War as a result of trying to prevent war! For only with war could one contemplate the ocean-to-ocean smorgasbord of corpses the carrion-eaters so eagerly anticipated. Death after all was their due. It was unfair to apply morality to them, especially if it demanded abstinence from feeding on the aftermath of death. If those stupid land animals, like the elephants and turtles making those battle plans, were so short-sighted as to think they could control the birds of prey, they had better think again! Humans being victimized? People circumscribed in their right to besmirch the globe? Governments prevented from waging global thermonuclear war? Preposterous! The creatures would never, ever succeed! But just to make sure, the birds of prey must do everything to sabotage the idiotic battle plans. Human beings—fellow eaters of dead flesh—must be helped in their hour of revolution with counter-revolution. The humans will triumph! But of course, the humans must never know who was helping them, or why. Humans had never shown much friendship or sympathy to birds of prey even though—*by vulture!*—they ought to realize how much was held in common!

As far as that "final war" that would destroy all life, *baldeagledash!* Wild exaggeration fostered by knobby-kneed cowards. On the other hand, a few good, big wars was a stench of a different odor. Humans would always engage in that kind of foul action, with its delicious just dessert—carrion.

"Thank you, brothers, for your valuable assistance. Have a burnt offering!"

Chernobyl & the Lie

APRIL 27

On the twenty-seventh day, the turtle-generals gathered to assess and relay to Old Eddie the results of the attacks around the globe. They learned through fast-flying birds of a fantastic operation the day before at a remote location in the Ukraine, at a place named Chernobyl. Rats—long hated by the humans—had not been able to attend the Congress, but they had heard what had been advocated, so they came up with a plan of their own. It was bold and it was dangerous, but the accomplishment would sing in the history books of animals for years to come.

The rats—or ratz as they called themselves, hissing the "z," mean and proud—hesitated outside the high fence with the barbed wire topping until their leader, Yuri, the nastiest of the bunch, said: "C'mon guys! It's a piece of cake." Smoothing his slick gray whiskers, he drooled. A nuclear power plant! The opportunity of a lifetime! A chance to get back at the "Big Uglies," the name the ratz had given people, those lousy killers of every relative and friend he'd ever had. Until now the only thing a lowly rat could do to get back at them was knock over a garbage can and make the big uglies pick up the slop with their bare hands—Level F Basic Training for a rat. Or jump from the shadows and frighten somebody—Level E, a little higher, though if the target were infirm, old, or pregnant, worth more—perhaps a Level D or C. Of course, the time Yuri attempted to stampede some circus elephants into a crowd of Big and Little Uglies could probably have earned him a Level B or A for sure. But ratz weren't mice. The elephants had refused to take the bait. The stampede fizzled. A big fat goose egg for that one. Just as well. If anyone had died in that stampede, he'd never have been chosen to head this, the most exciting adventure of his life.

Yuri rubbed his paws together and smacked his lips. He could hardly wait. The head rat, Vassily, had fired them up with a wonderful speech, and Yuri was determined to do his best. "If the superpowers recognize the potential danger of nuclear power plant disasters, they'll be less likely to risk nuclear war. Your job is to make them recognize that."

Pasha, a pudgy rat, stuck out his lip, glancing first at the plumes of smoke swirling above the tall white towers beyond the barbed wire fence, then at Yuri. He had none of Yuri's street smarts. He'd lived a rather sheltered life in an abandoned tenement, away from his more adventuresome sewer-dwelling cousins. His teeth weren't any sharper than his wits. He'd been pushed into volunteering by some older, bigger ratz with better things to do than chase after a nuclear power plant. "Why me?" he whined.

"You should be honored," chided some true believers.

"I suppose so, but somehow I'm not. No, I'm not. Not one little bit..."

"Oh, shut up," said someone.

As Yuri began to cut through the brittle metal fence with his razor-sharp teeth, Pasha and his twenty-two confederates reluctantly joined him. In a matter of teeth-baring moments, they had chewed through several metal links, the split ends glistening with saliva. Suddenly a bell rang. A light flooded the roadway parallel to the fence. Blood splurted from a rat named Vlad. Whirling, he nipped at the wretch's tail he thought had shoved him, then leapt through the opening, barely ahead of the others. They dashed across a parking lot, past some sort of outpost, drawing up short behind a two-tiered turbine building. There, in the open space across from a low, oblong structure resembling a breadbox, a few men milled about, smoking cigarettes and talking. Yuri pointed to the boxy building.

"The big milk bottles—the white ones—are back that way," whispered Pasha. "Wouldn't we rather be there?"

"Big milk bottles?" asked Yuri, then realizing Pasha meant the cooling towers. "You jerk, that's where the wasted hot water turns to steam. Who cares about the stupid towers? Didn't you hear the generals say we're to neutralize the reactor control building?"

Pasha hadn't paid much attention to what the generals said. He looked at the towers again. How could one disregard those huge structures? They dwarfed the small houses, farm buildings, and trees in the fields, like the refrigerator full of cheese his friend Alexei had once shown him. "If we could only find a way to open the door," said Alexei, "we'd have a mountain of cheese. We'd be set for life." Like the refrigerator, those towers were impossible to climb. Yuri had figured that out. Pasha looked at him, eyes shining, faith in his leader renewed.

Another rat, this one grey with brown spots and named Ivan, spoke up. "It's too well guarded."

"I don't care if it has a thousand attack dogs," said Yuri, sharpening his teeth on a rock. "Do I hear any more objections?"

"Couldn't we eat first?" asked Pasha, rubbing his stomach.

Yuri looked at Pasha as if he would snap off his head at any moment. He hadn't eaten in hours. "All right," he said, leading the way. "Last one to the garbage cans is a dirty cat."

Before any of the Big Uglies could react, the ratz had carted off pieces of fruit, grains, and rotting meat. Unable to find any trees to picnic under, they flopped on the warm ground near two steel doors marked: "Reactor Containment Building Number 2."

Light yellow ferrets and dark hoot owls swooped down at him from every direction. They had him cornered. They were going to tear him apart.

Pasha awoke with a start and looked around him. How long had he slept? He wiggled his nose and perked up his ears. This plant might be dangerous, but could a place without any real owls or ferrets be all bad?

The moon was halfway across the sky as the troop started out again, Yuri in the lead, Pasha bringing up the rear. Pasha looked around nervously at the other fellows with their large teeth and battle scars from earlier confrontations with humans and other animals. His only scar was a pimple above his right eye. But that would likely end tonight. I'll be lucky to escape with my life, he thought. Why would any sensible rat chase after anything but the three essentials—food, family, and decent housing?

They reached the control building. Two humans stood talking in front of a door. Careful, signaled Yuri, in an age-old shift of the paw, but Yuri wasn't careful enough.

An object sailed from the hand of a monster in a white plastic suit with a see-through face mask and flew by Pasha's head. Another monster opened fire from the front. Before the ratz could scatter, various objects zinged through the air. Ivan hit the ground. Pasha almost slipped in some goo on the ground and fell near Ivan, but managed to keep going.

"Run, feet, run," shrieked Pasha, darting this way and that. He must escape, but where? Anywhere. A roar filled his ears. He stopped, then realized it was only the sound of his breathing. He sniffed about. No one. Especially no white-suited monsters. He sat down, mopped his brow, and looked around. He was in a small darkened "L" between two outbuildings. All was silent.

No way to regroup now. The plan was dead. How will I ever get back to the tenement alive? Oh well, it wasn't much of a life anyway in a world that knew nothing about his feelings, where bigots were always saying, "My God, it's a rat," or "Eeek, kill the damn thing!" Was it his fault he hadn't been endowed with long graceful gliding legs like cats and dogs, but only with short, stubby ones that made him slither like an overgrown snake?

Who in his right mind would ask to be born a rat, anyway? Why couldn't the Big Uglies look past appearance and into the soul of a creature the way Pasha had heard spiritual people did? A spiritual person looking to the inner self finds incredible riches, power, beauty, and peace, more lasting than one could ever find in worldly desires. But the part Pasha liked best was that once the inner self was tapped, a person could realize a spiritual link-up with every other thing on earth. Who knows, perhaps even ratz?

Pasha shivered. Why think like a philosopher if I'm going to act like a fighter? His ears picked up the pre-arranged signal to regroup. Yuri was alive, well, and roaring! Let him wait. He slowly followed the sound of the call. What if ratz carried diseases? So did humans. Besides, what rat had ever threatened to blow up the world?

The others were already gathered at the control building as Pasha ambled up, leisurely picking his teeth. "Hi, guys," he said. "You sure did get here fast."

"Start digging," ordered Yuri, shoving Pasha.

"Me, dig? Where?" He looked at his soft, clean paws.

"Over there!" Yuri pointed to two brutes, Grobonov and Gromov, busily scraping bits of concrete from a small hole, heaping them into a pile.

Pasha made some shoveling motions, but Gro and Grom, as they were called, did the bulk of the work. When all was ready, everyone crept single file through the hole. Pasha, thankful to be last in line, wasn't anxious to see what lay on the other side of the black hole. He'd heard stories about strange, dangerous, and enormous things from bugs, lice, and termites who'd lived at nuclear facilities. He remembered the turtle-general's instructions: "Un-work everything. Open valves that are closed. Close valves that are open. Turn on switches that are off. Turn off switches that are on. Levers set low, turn high. Levers set high, turn low. Flip switches, push buttons. Stop and start everything in reverse. Gnaw through conduits—not enough to electrocute yourselves—but enough to foul up the turbines and the reactor thermocouples that regulate heat activity in the core." But if everyone thought the plant operators were going to sit by as their careers, hopes, and nuclear dreams were smashed, they were wrong. Ivan was dead and if someone didn't help soon, the monsters in white suits would do them all in.

Enter the anopheles mosquitoes.

"The anoph-who?" Pasha had blurted out, upon first hearing the name.

"The anopheles are carriers of a dread virus known as encephalitis, or equine encephalitis, because horses are the usual victims," the turtle-general had explained. "People have stronger antibodies than horses, but they can develop a kaleidoscope of symptoms after coming in contact with an infected mosquito or bird."

"What symptoms?"

"Nasty headaches, rashes, convulsions, vomiting, and, in rare cases, unconsciousness and death. But lethargy is the usual reaction. That's why encephalitis is called a form of sleeping sickness."

"We don't need the help of any stupid mosquitoes," the ratz shouted. But the turtle-general prevailed, enrolling thousands of the anopheles from swamps along the Onepier River near Chernobyl and the breeding grounds of Ukrainian horses, who were glad to see them go. And it was a good thing, thought Pasha. The mosquitoes had begun biting men as they went in and out of the plant ten days earlier. The incubation period was five to fifteen days, the greatest danger occurring in ten days. The ratz invaded the nuclear plant at midnight of the tenth day, dangerously close to the time the rook had said the terrorists planned to nuke Syria.

Bird spies had heard the men complaining about "a damn lot of mosquitoes, especially for April," but none suspected that thanks to some agreeable viruses that didn't care who they infected, the odds against catching encephalitis so far from any swamp had been overcome.

The mosquitoes had to be rewarded for this "kamikaziq-uito" mission, of course. Because of temperature changes and long distances, they would not be able to return to the swamp. So extra breeding space was offered. With this added room, the anopheles, instead of merely being equal with the Culex and Aedes mosquito families, could rise to become the Ukraine's largest mosquito family. Those who died for the cause would be the patriarchal stingers of a new race. Another reward was respect: creatures who had never experienced anything but a swat and a smack now received praise. "Incredible! Those damn mosquitoes are finally doing something useful."

The wild ponies of the Ukraine, once bred by Cossacks, had objected, fearing they might be bitten to extinction by the swollen flying hordes, but the horses' objections were overridden.

That the mosquitoes had done something useful was apparent the moment Pasha and the other ratz entered the control room. A sandy-haired man stared confusedly at a visual CRT display. A red-faced chap zigzagged about the room like a drunk. A slightly built fellow slumped over a panel of flashing yellow and white lights, as though trying to squeeze his nose through the eye of the computer.

Other people, although alert, fought swarms of mosquitoes that buzzed about. Pasha clapped his paws over his ears to stifle what sounded like a million saws buzzing at once.

Then some of the mosquitoes began divebombing the ratz. Everyone dove for cover, except Yuri. He stood his ground, signaling friendship by yelling the code words: "Mosquitoes forever!"

Hearing this, some of the insects intercepted their stinging mates, but not before a shiny white rat nicknamed Gap-Tooth collapsed with eight or ten bites to his face and belly.

"Is he dead?" asked Yuri, nudging Gap-Tooth with his nose.

The mosquitoes swarmed about, confused. "We've never bitten a rodent," said one of the mosquitoes.

"Maybe he just fainted," added another. "By the time you're through in here, he should be fine."

"But we must hurry," said a third. "If someone's smelled a rat, and sounded the alarm, the attackers will—"

"What do you mean—smelled a rat?" asked an angry Yuri

"Uh, sorry."

"No sensitivity—none at all," said young Adam.

"Please, move quickly."

"All right, all right!" Yuri ordered. "First, let's help Gap-Tooth."

Pasha and a black sewer dweller named Subterranean Joe carried their wounded colleague to a white equipment control console and rested him on top of it.

Now everyone leapt to the heart of the plant's operations—the panels and fixtures.

"One false move here and—bam—everything comes tumbling down," said Yuri.

Pasha's mouth dropped open. He'd been briefed along with the others on what to expect, but nothing had prepared him for this: giant couplings, computer boards, screens flashing numbers and lights, and a staggering array of switches, knobs and buttons. "If our leader Vassily the Wise, could see this," Pasha called to no one in particular, "he'd do more than bob and weave. He'd get dizzy." His brain spun as the insects buzzed about, men ran amok, and red lights flashed "Security" and "Do not enter." He covered his head to shut out the din of the alarm bells, having flashbacks to the time when the tenement he'd lived in had been blown up by a wrecker and he'd barely escaped. But not for long.

Yuri spurred everyone on. Up the sideposts they scrambled to the control panels. While one rat pushed, another pulled at a closed switch, opening it. A third and fourth rat did the opposite to an open switch—one pulling, the other pushing it closed. One broke a small glass temperature meter with his paw, screeching as the blood spurted. Others stepped over the keyboards of the CRT terminal. A succession of confusing responses appeared on the monitor.

Subterranean Joe tried to flip a switch. Getting no reaction, he flopped over on his stomach causing it to go "off" and "on" as an indicator light blinked.

"Hey, it's my job to flip things, not yours," objected a rat named Flip.

"Shut up and help me," said Joe, struggling to release his head from between two switches. "I'm stuck."

A rat steps over a keyboard of a CRT terminal.

"What's next?" said Flip, calling to Spit-Patoii and two other rodents. They managed to extract Joe, then set about serious work. Locking their tails together they produced a windmill effect and wrapped themselves around the dial, causing it to move counterclockwise. Other ratz joined them, grunting and wheezing. Some dials moved; some did not. A few attackers gave up trying, leaping willy-nilly across the boards, seeking smaller, more tempting targets. They found them in the various black and green buttons and pushed them with abandon.

Bells rang. Human reinforcements arrived. They lit into the ratz with broom handles, wadded-up newspapers, and sticks. Others charged them with strange metallic objects resembling video game joy sticks that reached their targets with deadly accuracy. Yuri managed to duck one of the objects, but a companion to his left got it full force and fell over, blood oozing from his head. Dazed, Yuri signaled his cohorts to follow him. They clamored over the top of the computer board, slid down the back, and began chomping at the wires leading to the in-reactor thermocouples. Sparks flew, then crackled, as if trying to speak.

The men in the white suits were now hot on their trail. They poked and jabbed away. Ceasing the attack, Yuri broke into a run, stopping only briefly to signal retreat to his cadre. They almost knocked him down as they dashed out as fast as their little feet could carry them, the white-suited monsters on their heels.

It was then that Pasha performed an act so brave that never again could a tenement rat be called a "safe, secure lazy critter." Turning on his tormentors, he snarled and hissed. His pursuers skidded to a halt. Without thinking, he pounced onto the shoe of the nearest Big Ugly and chomped through his sock, sinking his pointed teeth into the soft flesh just above his ankle. Yelping, the man tripped and tumbled over the man directly behind him.

But now the other men screamed for revenge. They swung at Pasha, but they were too late. He had accomplished his mission. The confusion had allowed his confederates to get back through the hole in the wall where they'd entered. Just as the group of Big Uglies swung at him and Pasha thought he was trapped for sure, a group of mosquitoes dove at them in one long stinging column, and he was able to scramble through the hole to safety.

The group was barely outside the barbed wire fence when a series of explosions lit up the sky. Pasha glanced over his shoulder. Flames licked the sky, casting everything in an eerie glow. There was no time to waste. They must throw as much distance between themselves and the plant as they could before the meltdown.

"The beauty of it," bragged Vassily, the head rat debriefer, "is that no one but the plant operators will ever know the truth. For who among the Ukraine's sober scientists, engineers, and rulers will risk ridicule or commitment to a mental hospital by suggesting that the greatest nuclear accident of the century was caused by rats? No, they'll say, 'It's computer malfunction, a stuck valve, instrument failure.' Or they'll locate some lowly scapegoats and say they were on drugs, or drinking. Or just resort to that old cop-out—human error. But rats—never. You are to be commended, Yuri."

"I stand ready to serve," said Yuri, puffing out his chest. "I'd like to sabotage a bomb assembly plant next. How 'bout it?"

"Patience, patience," said Vassily. "I give the orders around here."

As for Pasha, he mopped his brow, wondering why he felt so overheated and why he seemed to be shedding his coat rather early. Then he melted quietly into the background, glad to be going home.

The Sea Party

APRIL 28

Even though events so far had involved animals or birds, the creatures of the deep weren't unaware of what was happening. For who but they among the inhabitants of land, sea, and air knew more about underwater nuclear tests and the dumping of poisons into rivers and oceans that had caused the extinction, or near extinction, of so many species? Blood flowed around the aquatic world from these incursions, causing gnashing of teeth and rippling of fins from the Arctic to Antarctica, from the Bering Sea to the Indian Ocean, and back again. The sufferers, unable to see where they were swimming for the carnage, longed to escape. But to where?

Even good news was contaminated! For when tuna, clams, mussels, and oysters reported temporarily reduced catches, meaning they might not become extinct, rejoicing quickly turned to despair when they learned the world wasn't turning vegetarian; man simply didn't want to eat his own poisons now contained in fish food! Good news for man, but what about fish?

Did man think tuna, mussels, or goldfish had no feelings?

"Who the deuce are humans to think they're the only ones who bleed or screech with pain?" Hota, a spindly, professorial sea turtle asked his fellow turtles off Land's End, England. "Does not every sea creature try to escape his tormentors and live another day?" He stretched his neck. A pair of spectacles that had washed up on the shore one day sat awkwardly on his face. "Well, don't they?" he repeated.

Nods of approval. Low grunting noises.

Hota looked down from a rock atop his island home off Land's End, called Ocean's First Gulp. "We think it's a denial of equal protection under the Queen's law that people kill animals and fish and eat them. They kill other people, too, but they don't eat them. If a human can eat an animal, why not a person? What's so bloody special about people? But what can one expect from those who form sex education protest committees to prevent their children from learning how to mate properly? Would we ever form a committee to prevent spawning?"

The assembled creatures—diamondback terrapins, snapping turtles, tortoises, loggerheads, and various other sea turtles—vegetarian all—clapped their flippers. They had gathered from far and wide because Hota, one of their own and the most renowned living historian, who had long lived on this British island, had been named to head the English aquatic side of the Revolt of the Animals. His counterparts in the Mediterranean, the Baltic, and elsewhere were also hard at work.

All present wondered what Hota was planning. For the moment, as stragglers to the meeting "helloed" from atop far-cresting waves, they were content to listen as Hota expounded on his favorite topic: history.

Hota looked over the crowd, biding his time. He wanted everyone to arrive before dropping the bombshell—the news of their dangerous assignment.

"Whereas in the past the eating and killing by humans was selective," said Hota, squinting nearsightedly, "now the slaughter threatens to become universal. Such democracy—where we all may die—we need like a hole in our shells."

Urkle, urkle, urkle sounds echoed about the inlet. Hota undid a large sheaf of papers held together with reeds, inscribed "Sea History, Volume 23" on its faded bamboo cover. He turned to a blank page. A cod named Tibby began inscribing his words on the pages with a pointed pheasant quill dipped in blue dye from the coral reefs about the island.

"In the old days," said Hota, as some of the visitors flipped onto their backs to sun their bottoms, "each sea creature kept largely to himself, consumed by the quest for food and water, there being few, if any, so-called 'oceanic' questions to flood their minds. That fish, mammals, and reptiles all shared the same living space—water—meant no more to them than lions and people felt kinship because they both occupy the land. But gradually, after certain disasters, aquatic consciousness was, so to speak, raised. The creatures came to feel a common unity."

There were more than a few upside-down puzzled glances.

"What I bloody well mean," said Hota, supporting his frail body on a carved English walking stick, "is that the slogan 'Every fish for himself' that one finds in the history books—roughly, volumes one through twelve—was replaced around the middle of fish history with the slogan: 'We must form schools'—the first time fish traveled together in large numbers for safety's sake. But the fish found that although the schools provided *some* defense against attack, the new threats went beyond the safety of this or that particular school, and involved us *all.* This new awareness didn't find expression in a motto, however, until a few years ago, in the beginning of volume twenty-three, when we first heard the famous phrase: 'All must live, or all will die."

"I can't write as fast as you talk," complained the cod.

"Slower than a stream, but faster than a creek," said Hota, slowing up. "That catchy slogan, 'All must live, or all will die,' has gained currency, except with the octopuses who live off in the dark and don't give a tentacle what goes on in the light world above them."

"Hurry up," said a group of turtles.

Hota sighed. It wasn't easy to be a historian. "I'm obliged to omit some history I wanted to share with you," he said.

A pleased *urkle* from the front row.

"But one thing I must say: we've all credited the humpback whale with the expression 'All must live, or all will die.' I sent them a message several weeks ago—apparently the first time anyone bothered to ask them—and they said it was the mighty blue whales, not they, who dreamed up that ringing cry of unity."

Eyes popped. A sea turtle named Clem fell backwards into the water.

"Hardly the humpback's fault they didn't originate what we thought they had," said a loggerhead named Sharf.

"Quite true, Hota, but I should have known," a tortoise said. "Although the humpbacks' music makes the waves jump, the blues are the geniuses—the biggest creatures on the face of the planet, the smartest, yet the most kind of beasts."

"Rubbish!" snorted a speckled sea gull as she alighted on a rock. "If the whale is so smart, how come he can't fly?"

"For the same reason you can't spout," said the sea turtle who had fallen into the drink as he climbed onto a sandbar.

"Now leave us alone. Hota's on a roll, and I want to hear what happened next."

"And so you shall," said Hota, shooing the sea gull as it tried to eat the cod scribe. "With this newfound unity, *word* bubbled upward some storms ago from small fish to big ones, from the big fish to the turtles, turtles to birds and birds to elephants. And that *word* was fear. We didn't hide the *word* from one another, as we might have in our most isolated, suspicious, distrustful past, or muddy the water with confusing messages. No. Now we were united, and we let the world know! And lo and behold, we heard more clearly than we had ever seemed to hear in our disorganized past. And sure enough, it wasn't many storms later that the *word* gurgled back down to us; and it was *relax*, the Congress had met. The humans' war machine was about to be washed up, beached, sunk, or however which way you wish to drown it. And when they heard this delightful news they held a party."

"Oh, wowee! Can we go?" asked a young turtle named Zoot.

"The party's over," said Hota.

"Then let's have a party of our own!"

"Who ever heard of a turtle partying?" said the young turtle's mother. "Where did I go wrong that this tad should want to party?"

"Wait!" shouted Clem, Zoot's great uncle, though he was

but fourteen, "I don't see why we can't have a—." But he leaned too far and again fell into the drink.

"To be sure, festivities are a waste of time," said Hota, a sour expression on his wrinkled face. He was in too poor shape to party himself, his body wasted from years of historical research, writing, and thought. "But Arabus," he said, pointing to a large green turtle in earnest conversation with a salamander, "was invited to the gala and observed firsthand who might help us in our assignment."

"And what's that?" asked Zoot's mother.

"Later," said Zoot. "First, I want to hear about the party."

"I don't think Arabus wants to bore us with news of the party. He just wants to let us know who can help us, and who can't. Isn't that right?"

"Oh I don't know about that," said Arabus, not taking the hint. "You see, it was the first party I've ever attended. And I'm one to agree with Zoot—I'd like to attend another." He looked about good-naturedly, finding friendly faces. "Ah, what a party! Right smack in the middle of the Atlantic. Well, maybe not quite the middle, but certainly near the middle. Perhaps not more than a few hundred miles off—"

"Oh, get on with it," said Zilch, Zoot's sister.

"Ahem, well yes, you see the affair was full of song and dance. It began with the flutefish and trumpetfish mimicking the woeful attempts of humans to imitate the sounds of nature with artificial contrivances they call clarinets, violins, and pianos. Why, a bird needs nothing *mechanical* to trill its lovely sounds."

"That's for sure," whistled a passing mockingbird, rattling off the sounds of three different birds, a jackhammer, and a steam whistle before being shushed.

"I especially like the sounds of the humpbacks," said Arabus, shifting his large body to one side. "Until now, I thought their sounds had no meaning."

"They do?" asked someone.

"Oh, yes," said Arabus. "Some are to fool people. Humans spend endless hours trying to dissect the humpbacks' sounds, never suspecting they're imitating the people studying them—laughing, crying, singing, slobbering, sighing—and if you pardon me, breaking wind. It was quite a party all right."

"Seems more like speech-making than partying to me," said Zoot's mother.

"Then you don't want to hear about the marlin," said Arabus. "They didn't make any speeches, but shot through the air, flipping backward and forward, daring humans to try and catch them! And longtailers – the moray eels and oarfish – they did some kind of exotic tail dance. Looked X-rated to me. But to tell the truth, I can't say for sure. I was too busy fighting off a large, slimy creature trying to turn me into a bowl of soup. My hosts finally dispatched it."

Sighs of relief.

"Ah yes, and then I got a kick out of some swordfish who staged mock battles. Picture this: One swordfish representing people, another swordfish the sea – attacking each other with their sharp blades. After each thrust strikes home, a seahorse umpire cries, 'Victory!' for whichever swordfish wins a particular battle. But after each battle, both winners and losers rise to the surface of the water to illustrate that in a real war, especially the whopper the major powers are always threatening each other with, there'll be no winners, only losers."

"That was a *political* party!" shouted Zoot's mother.

"I still like it!" said Zoot.

"You're not too young to hear the frightening part, are you, my boy?"

Zoot moved back a pace, bumping into Zilch. The two embraced each other.

"A scary vibration passed through the water," began Arabus. "Fearful sharks. Expecting a blood bath, the tuna dived for cover, but instead of sharks two huge blue whales rolled out like thunder from the north. The tuna knew they were safe, but not the krill, the small phosphorescent shrimp-like food whales love. The krill fled, but they need not have, for the whales were there not to eat, but to dance!"

"A mammal the size of a mountain can dance?" asked Zoot.

"Ah, but size is not the key, nor age, but ability and will," Arabus said. "To see Heoo, the male, and Oola, the female, is to witness genuine underwater ballet. True, they displaced five hundred tons of water. But ah, how they danced, their gait more complicated than the two-step, more stately than hard rock. Such rhythm and body commitment I'd never seen. Up and down, in and around, a smooth watery path—"

Zoot tried to imitate the sounds.

"Swing your partner. Nudge her 'round and 'round, and back where you've started."

Zoot tried to imitate the movements as Arabus said:

Then Heoo burst into song:

"Let's give the humans thirty whacks,
Lay them flat on their backs,
Can't bomb us from that position,
Making a laughing stock of atomic fission!"

And everyone joined in:

"*Blup, blup, blup*."

Oola sang the next stanza:

"Let's give the humans sixty whacks,
Nail them down with enormous tacks,
Who cares then if they yell 'Bombs away!'
Let them scream, 'We've won the day!'"

And then they repeat the chorus:

"*Blup, blup, blup*."

Zoot's eyes widened.

"And again marlin shot through the air. Mackerel performed

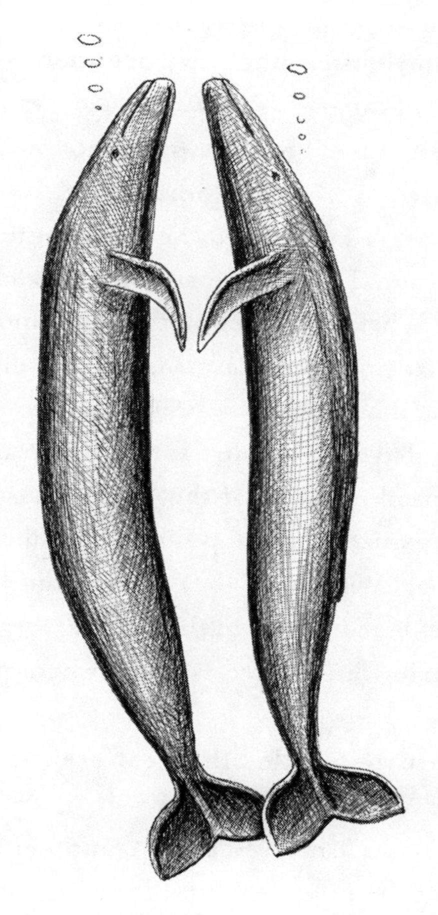

Oola sang the next stanza:

"Let's give the humans sixty whacks,

Nail them down with enormous tacks,

Who cares then if they yell 'Bombs away!'

Let them scream, 'We've won the day!'"

figure eights, and lobsters lined up sixteen abreast for what they called a claw-claw can-can. Amazing," said Arabus, looking at his toes, "at least to me. I have claws, but not much of a can."

"Then improvise," said Zoot. "Watch!" Nudging the younger members of the crowd, he led them in a kind of impromptu can-can. They all joined toes and kicked their feet, twelve abreast. What they lacked in skill, they more than made up for with gusto and enthusiasm, as Arabus bellowed the musical sounds he'd heard fifty fathoms below to urge them on. Some even wiggled their tails in a sort of bump and grind.

The surprised mothers of the young ones dancing with Zoot finally organized their opposition after the last chorus of "*Blup, blup, blup.*" With howls they charged the group, forcing the end of the dance. Some of the fathers who had been urging their offspring on, also received angry beratings from their mates.

While the turtles settled their differences, Arabus concluded: "That's all she wrote!"

"Troublemaker!" shrieked a young mother as she tried to poke Arabus in the nose. But just in the nick of time, Arabus retracted his head into his shell.

"Thank you very much," said Hota to the now headless shell. Then to the others: "I find the role played by the blues especially interesting. They not only originated the unity slogan, but they have a new way of generating enthusiasm. I think they're the natural choice to supervise the big job assigned to the sea creatures—"

"Which is?"

"To organize and supervise the destruction of the underwater cables, which is one way the humans carry communications between countries."

"Why can't we do the job ourselves?"

"Really! Give me credit! How touchy you all are! You know if any of us tried to dive to the ocean floor, our ears would pop, or one of those slimy dark creatures who tried to behead Arabus would snap first and ask questions later."

"We see your point," said a terrapin named Softjoints, "but what good are the whales for that sort of work?"

"No good, directly. The electric rays, the most shocking fish in the ocean, must do the job."

A shiver and a moan.

"The electric rays, known to all, and universally feared."

"But they're secretive, solitary, and treacherous," objected Softjoints.

"Precisely. The strength, mobility, and organizational talents of the blues will be tested to the utmost in their attempt to make the rays work! Those cables must explode like fireworks!"

"Senõr," said a Spanish snapping turtle named Juan, "a blue whale – she once try to bite off my head."

"I see you're still quite attached to it," said Hota. "Now if you don't mind, we must notify the blue—"

"Just a flippin' minute," Clem cried. "Softjoints and Joan have a point."

"Juan, not Joan," said the Spanish turtle. "I'm not a female."

"Sorry, but I'm far-sighted. I have a hard time telling who is which, or what is what. We turtles never were great at distinguishing males from females at more than two meters away."

"*Urkle*!" from the crowd.

Lest he open up a three to five day debate, Hota proceeded as though the concern was over the whales. "I'll name some potential organizers, and if you find someone more qualified than the blues, so be it. But let's move quickly. The sun is beginning to set. I'll start counting and—"

"Hold it!" shouted Clem, fighting not to fall off a large clump of floating moss. "I'll count potential organizers, and you name them!"

"Must you?" sighed Hota. Did his cousins on the other side of the Atlantic have such organizational problems? Hota's ancestors had lived on this island from time immemorial and having imbibed of the mainland and its ways, he knew a certain amount of eccentricity had to be tolerated if one were to conceive of one's self as truly English. Still, how this temporary resident eccentric, Clem, had found his way over the water from Scotland without drowning was a real mystery. "You may count," said Hota, "but keep a mind to what you're doing."

"No problem." said Clem, waving the speaker on."Worry about yourself. One..."

"I must start with the lancelet," said Hota, "historically the mother and father of all backboned creatures, though oddly enough it never advanced beyond a primitive state."

"Some never learn," said Clem. "Two."

"The sponges. No backbone at all. They couldn't lead us to the watering hole, let alone the cables."

"That's for sure. Three."

"Keep counting."

"Three–four?"

"The dolphins and the porpoises. Certainly intelligent, but how can you trust a creature who, when the humans say, 'Jump,' ask 'How far?'"

"*Urkle, urkle.*"

"Eat cereal?" asked Clem.

"Are you hard of hearing as well as blind?" asked Hota. "Just one, two, three, four."

"No need to get sassy because you're using all those big words," said Clem. "One through four—there!"

"The humpback, great sperm, Greenland, and sulphur bottoms—all marvelous whales, but were they the ones who dreamed up the great slogan, 'All must live, or all will die'?"

"Or," he said as he looked at Zoot and Zilch, "did they form a political party in the middle of the ocean?"

A resounding chorus of no's.

Clem squirmed about, afraid he'd run out of toes before Hota ran out of candidates. He turned to his other foot, started counting. "One, two, and–"

"Stop!" commanded Hota. "Just two right now—the halibut and tuna. Decent fish, but too unreliable."

"You never know whether they will be swimming or will wind up in somebody's cook pot."

"Three, and—"

"Just three. The scorpion fish, frightening and trusted by no one."

"Not even by their relatives?" asked the cod-scribe.

"Obviously, we're not talking about relatives. If you'll just do your job—" he said, looking sternly at the cod.

"Please continue," said the cod, trying to hide its yellowish face behind its quill pen.

"Four!" said Clem.

"Four. The sharks. Bright but bloodthirsty."

"Five," said Clem, a look of alarm spreading over his face. "Did I say five? I only have four toes on each foot. Somebody help me. I'm going to be killed. Something's slithering up my body! And me with my head all exposed! There's something—but I can't...it's oh my, oh gee—Whew! It's okay, folks.

False alarm. Just a...heh, heh slimy stick." He threw the scaly twig in the ocean then popped into the water, his face red with shame.

Hisses and boos greeted Clem's departure. Intelligent turtles weren't supposed to mistake sticks for enemies. But Hota, seeing a way to turn this event to advantage, yelled, "Stop! This fallen Ridgeway has taught us a lesson."

A loggerhead about to box Clem's ears stopped in mid-stroke.

"He's taught us how the most innocent thing can seem frightening, or the most frightening thing may reveal itself as benign."

Perplexed expressions.

"Don't you see?" said Hota, adjusting his glasses. "The whopping madness the humans propose fits either category. It not only seems horrible, it *is* horrible! But because the humans propose it, or rather, do nothing to stop it, they must know what happens after the final blow-up. Will everything be washed away? Or will power return again to those who held sway millennia ago, the animals and fish? And if the power returns to us, will we be ready to handle it?"

The sea creatures looked at each other, fear blanching their faces. As for Clem, he stood transfixed in the water. How had Hota transformed shame into insight? And stopped him from getting punched in the face, too!

"We may never know the answers to these questions," said Hota, mounting a high rock where he faced the setting sun, "but future generations will never forgive us for not trying." He raised a threatening fist into the wind, now blowing from the west. "The time for debate has ended; the hour for action has begun! I say, let's send word immediately! Tonight!"

The shouting roared over cascading waves. It was unanimous. The word was *action*!

Except for Clem, who was still too stunned to vote.

The blue whales found the call for assistance not entirely unexpected. They agreed to help immediately. Heoo and Oola were dispatched to rendezvous with the electric fish. The two mighty blues were on their way almost before the turtles broke camp an hour after dusk.

The Rays Charge

April 29

While the turtles talked, the electric rays, the highest voltage fish in the ocean, were having their own problems. The source of the difficulty arose years ago, when a baby electric fish had washed up on the shores of Newfoundland. A buzzard flying overhead in search of dinner, seeing the small round creature lying on the rocks, tried to take a bite out of it. Though just a baby, the electric ray produced enough of a shock to give the buzzard a jolt. In anger, the buzzard kicked the ray—and lo, the creature found himself back in the water—alive! The ray shouted a "thank you," but the buzzard didn't know what in a bloody gizzard the ray was talking about. Years later, that same electric ray became head of all the rays in the Atlantic Ocean. And that same buzzard, who couldn't believe the stupidity of the electric rays in naming him their patron saint, but determined to take advantage of a golden opportunity, sent a message from his rocky promontory in northwest Colorado:

> They would all find themselves washed up on
> the shore if they followed the crazy plan hatched
> by the elephants and the turtles.

Actually, the buzzard initially sent his message to the electric eels. But the electric eels explained they lived only in the rivers, such as the Orinoco and the Amazon. So it could not have been an electric eel who'd shocked the buzzard in the oceanic waters off Newfoundland. When the buzzard described the creature who had jolted him as grey in color and shaped like an upside-down dinner plate, the eels knew immediately he was describing an electric ray, also known as a torpedo ray.

When the rays finally got the message, they were miffed. Their patron saint hadn't even known who they were! But this made them all the more determined to do his bidding, on the grounds that compliance would make it impossible for him to ever mistake their identity again.

"Pure masochism. That's what it is," said Electric Andy, a hold-out against the majority view. "What good will it do for us to honor our saint, the buzzard, if we have the entire sea world against the humans?"

"We can deal with the other fish the way we've always dealt with them," said the ray's leader, Hot Flash Charlie, shooting a few jagged volts of red and orange into the placid blue water. Charlie was the one who long ago had been saved by the buzzard. Though now old and withered, he still had a few good zaps left, and he conserved them more.

"We can't hold off the entire ocean," argued Regulator Ralph, another dissenter in the group of a hundred. "Perhaps we could help in the battle, but charge for our services. No pun intended. We all know it's not easy to be a positively-charged fish in a neutral and indifferent world. If, say, other marine life were to obtain for us some of those wonderful cushions from sunken passenger ships and airplanes we love to rest on, would that be so bad?"

"Maybe...it all depends."

The rays argued, their plate-like bodies gliding to and fro like a sea full of china, their chattering punctuated by occasional bolts of electricity, as one ray or another made a particularly heated comment.

Then they reached their decision. The blue whales were at first surprised, then incensed, when they heard the disappointing news.

"You mean we came all this way for nothing?" Oola asked.

"We narrowly avoided explosive harpoons and a lethal stew of cast-off bomb materials, chemical wastes, and heavy metals getting here," said Heoo.

"Waste," Oola interrupted her mate, "deadly to us and to the entire planet nurtured by the sea."

"And you choose to ignore those dangers," Heoo sputtered, "because some oafish, stupid, self-serving, wicked, pusillanimous, foul-smelling, wretched, ignoramus buzzard tells you to?"

With each new put-down of their patron saint, the rays grew more and more angry. Before anyone realized it, and certainly before Hot Flash Charlie had the opportunity to organize any well-planned attack, a young hothead named Loose Wire Louie yelled, "Charge!" And in one of those almost instinctive moves that can't be explained, an entire crowd of rays jumped into the fray.

Never having been attacked by rays, Heoo underestimated the power of these living third rails. But Oola, who dove after spouting, assessed the deadly danger in an instant. Water was a powerful conductor of electricity – and the rays were smart enough to aim straight for Heoo's sensitive eyes and blow-hole. Oola screeched, turned, and rammed every ray in sight. Then, flicking her lateral tail at the other attackers approaching her spouse, she stunned them.

Seeing his mate slashing and tearing, Heoo became

alarmed. It was one thing for him to be under siege, but an attack on his mate, the mother of his children, was too much. He barreled his head against two of the aquatic vermin, then pitted his massive body against other unspeakables who thought to surprise Oola from below.

Falling rays soon littered the ocean. Two tuna and a mackerel, chancing by as the battle began, were lucky to escape with superficial wounds. But other fish, including a seedy-looking salmon and an aimless porpoise, weren't so lucky. They and others were rammed, eaten, or both.

Passing sharks, their teeth dripping with blood, urged the battlers on, but Electric Andy, whom Hot Flash Charlie with his dying breath had named his successor, ordered a halt.

Heoo, seeing Andy wave a white rock of surrender, was ready to call it quits, but Oola, angry and upset, wasn't. Heoo trilled a few sounds in her ear before she relented. The mighty blues swam gracefully together.

"First they fight us, now they embrace," sneered Electric Andy's peaceful friend, Regulator Ralph. "Don't those insufferable whales do anything but fight and make love?"

Blood, cartilage, and bone floated on the turbulent waters. The fifty or sixty survivors feared for their lives. They looked to Andy for guidance. He looked at their adversaries. "What... what exactly is it you want?" he asked, testing his newfound leadership role.

"Yes, now that you just about wiped us out," said Ampere Al, one of the first to charge.

"By blubber, we had no choice. You know that!" said Oola. "We waited patiently. The thanks we got was an unprovoked assault! A fine way to treat emissaries. You can't blame us because so many of your gang—your followers—were killed, when you know full well—"

"Please! No moralizing!" said Andy, nervously flapping a fin. Oola had touched a raw nerve—the wrongness of the attack. Now, she was rubbing salt in the wound. Living in the ocean, as she did, there was more than enough salt *and* wounds to go around. "What do you persistent whales want?"

"You could start by letting us speak."

"How can we stop you?"

Oola cleared her throat and began haltingly. "We want you to know it was not our decision, but that of the Congress that you be called upon to do the dirty work."

"You're a born salesman," Heoo said sadly. "What an awful speech."

Several listeners inched backwards, looking for some means of escape.

"You think you can do better?" asked Oola. "Be my guest."

"The Congress passed over the sharks, the stingrays, and the swordfish, in favor of the brave rays," Heoo began. "If you cooperate, the other fish will provide extra rations. And we'll raid all the downed airplanes and sunken passenger ships we can find and get you the fine seat and deck cushions we all know you like to sleep on."

The rays looked at each other, attracted to the bounty in spite of themselves. Regrouping, they considered the inducements. After ten minutes, Electric Andy, sounding like an underwater lawyer, announced: "We accept your terms with one caveat. If there is any backlash, all the creatures of the sea must share the blame for retribution from the humans."

"Fair enough," agreed the whales, nodding. And so the deal was struck.

As the whales briefed the rays in their assignment, Ampere Al, who felt that Hot Flash Charlie should have passed on the leadership to him, gathered a renegade group. They didn't know how, but they would help the buzzard, and get the cushions. "Then we'll have the last laugh," they said. "In comfort."

Nibble Fish

APRIL 30

The next day the rays, escorted by the whales, swam north by northeast to "Cable City," site of two of the important trans-Atlantic oceanic cables. En route they encountered what they regarded as a bunch of cowards, the bonitos and halibut, who avoided them like a disease. Not so much from fear of being eaten, as fear of electrocution.

"We have an undeserved reputation for unfriendliness," said Ampere Al to his renegade followers. "Is it our fault that once many years ago, a ray accidentally shot a bolt at a newfound bonito friend, the same way a bear might squeeze a person to death out of enthusiasm? Instead of saying how unfriendly the bonito was to respond to an appeal of friendship by going belly up, everybody blames the poor ray—and every other ray for the next fifty years."

"Accidents do happen," said a ray. "It's so unfair to blame us all when ninety-nine percent of the time we have total control over our electrical impulses."

"I say let's get control over all the cushions!"

"Shh," cautioned Ampere Al, "We don't want Electric Andy to hear us plotting rebellion."

"They can't hear," said a brightly colored thinker named Shooter. "We're swimming a good fifty meters behind Andy. The question is, what kind of cushions do we want? Ship vs. airplane, long vs. short, rectangular vs. square, round or what?"

"Personally, I like the long deck chairs that fall off sinking cruise ships," said a family-minded ray. "I can fit my entire family—my mate, my three little ones, and even an aunt or uncle or two—on the long stretch of one of those cushions, and still have room for my in-laws far away from me on the short end of the cushions where the humans rest their heads."

"Oh, I don't know, I rather fancy the small square cushions from downed airplanes," said another ray, nose-diving to capture a minnow for dinner. "They provide privacy. For a bachelor like me they're just the ticket."

"You've both been bought off too cheaply," said Shocking Estelle, a female who had joined the group en route. "I'm old enough to recall stories of silk and satin cushions from the decks of the grand passenger liners like the *Titanic*. They don't make cushions like those anymore. Now they're all vinyl and plastic. One good, strong current, and poof—shredded wheat! Strictly for the birds!"

The rays continued talking until they reached the cable junction. Being there brought back memories of heavily clad humans with derricks, sea stations, and supply ships, unloading and splicing the cables on the murky sea floor many years ago. But this was the first time they had actually seen the cables, each about the size of an octopus tentacle, and just as black and shiny.

If an octopus had been attacked the way the rays attacked the cables, it would have had the good sense to collapse in a heap. Not so the cables. They absorbed the electrical shocks as if they'd been built for such treatment.

"I thought the turtles said the elephant figured three or four good knocks would take out these cables," said Electric Andy. "These are the toughest customers I've ever dealt with!"

"Call in the swordfish. They'll know what to do," suggested Regulator Ralph.

"Swordfish are great for cutting through kelp and seaweed, but they're useless against solid metal!" claimed a ray, throwing acid remarks at the suggested solution.

"Abab-absorb!" stuttered an elderly ray named Old Ohm, stroking his whiskers. "How could these c-c-cables c-contain

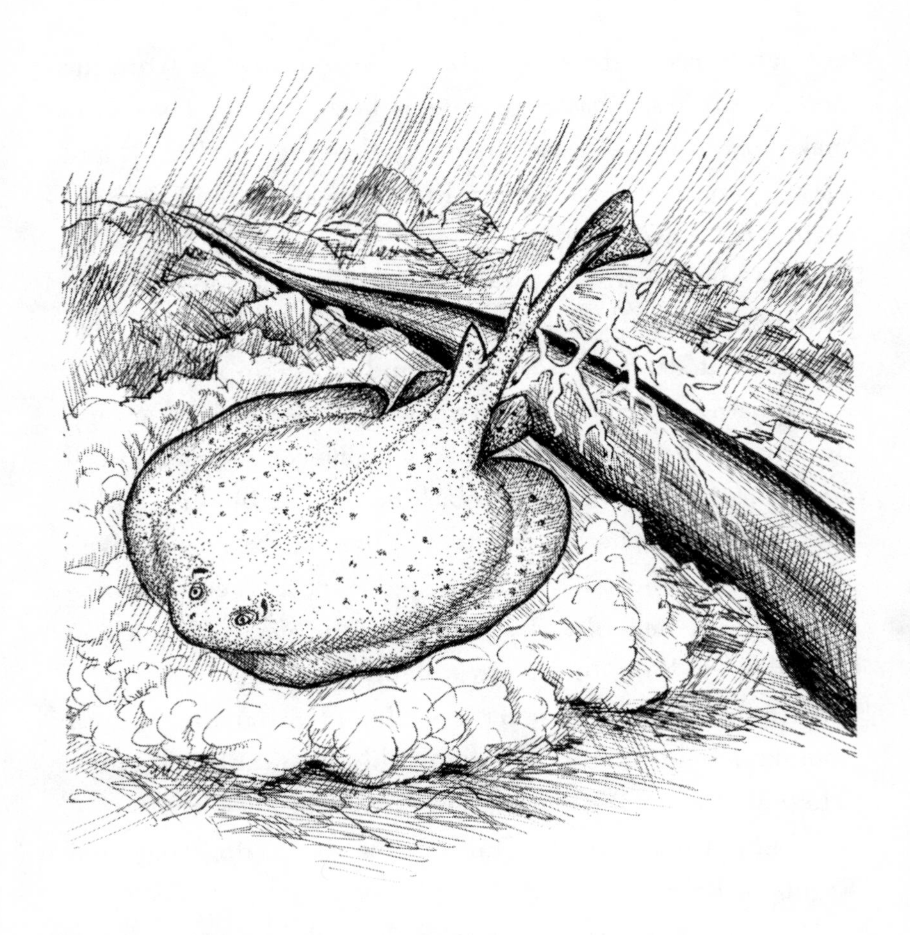

The cables absorbed the electrical shocks as if they'd been built for such treatment.

the thousands of s-strands the whales said they c-contain, if they were b-built solid?" To prove his point, he whacked one of the cables with his tail.

They all heard a ping, then something that sounded on the rebound like a pong.

"S-s-s-see?" he said turning with his withered dome to the crowd. "P-p-partially hollow."

"Thank you, Old Ohm," said Electric Andy, "but swordfish attacking these monster cables would be as useless as crabs attacking a shark. And don't suggest octopuses. They couldn't strangle these cables in a million years."

The only alternative was to ask Hota, the turtle-general in charge, what to do. But Hota claimed the surge of rebellious oceanic activity was taxing his historian abilities. He and the cod scribe Tibby must write several new chapters on sea history. A new turtle-general, a small but apparently sensible box turtle, Reginald Darby III, who lived above the white cliffs of Dover, had been named to take his place. Reginald wasted no time in analyzing the problem and sent word via seabirds to Heoo and Oola, who conveyed the message to the rays.

"The cable stretches from the United States to England, so why not survey the totality? The volcanic basalt, lava, or mud slides have weakened the line somewhere, I'm sure. Neutralize the cable at that location before human inspectors pop down to discover the stress and correct it."

"Splendid idea," said Regulator Ralph, doing a happy back-flip.

"Rotten idea. Too much work," said Ampere Al. "Let's go home."

"No sir. We do as the turtle says," ordered Andy, zinging a large, fiery bolt into the blue. All followed.

The rays charted the cable from a point east of New York City to west of Dover, concentrating on the deeper parts of the ocean where greater water pressure was more likely to cause stress, rather than on the continental shelves, where the cables sloped gently upward towards land.

The following afternoon they found a promising spot in the middle of the Atlantic, not far from where the famous fish party had been held. Oola, remembering when she and Heoo had danced and sang so wonderfully in their courtship days, nudged her mate affectionately, but was interrupted by cries from the rays. The rays indicated a place where an island had apparently risen from the ocean floor, then just as suddenly been sucked under the surface, causing numerous wiggle fissures.

"Drat," said Oola, "this had better be good."

"See," said Electric Andy, pointing, "the cable there seems to have lost some of its luster and looks slightly wobbly."

"Enough for us to do the job?"

"Can't say until we try."

For the next four days they tried. And tried again. Ray after ray, bolt after fiery bolt. They wore themselves out, recharged and tried again. But despite all their efforts and firing their most powerful shots, they were unable to cause a rupture – not even one tiny hole.

Finally, they lay spent and exhausted on a rocky outcropping. Ampere Al, totally worn out, moaned, "Let's go home."

"Yes," said Hotpoint Houdini, "and furthermore, we deserve the cushions from the next ship or plane that sinks for our stupendous effort."

"For more effort, I'll get you banana peels." said Oola.

"Worthless!"

"But only results will get you cushions."

"You insufferable— "

"Hold it," said Electric Andy, also tired and eager to go home, but doubting the whales would let them. "Tell you what. Let's say we check out some other part of the ocean where there are other cables?"

"Oh no you don't," said Hotpoint Houdini. "You're short-circuiting the issue."

After much discussion, the buck was again passed to Reginald Darby III. A few days later the seabirds delivered Reginald's message to the whales: "Use the nibble fish."

The whales, who had no teeth or gums, and who therefore never nibbled, asked, "What's a nibble fish?"

"They are creatures like the parrotfish, with little teeth. They nibble all day and all night," answered Darby. "Someone who takes small bites is a true nibbler. But actually, there are thousands of species who bite—some small and some medium size."

The whales conveyed the message to the rays.

"They don't understand," said the whales to the seabirds who conveyed the message to Reginald Darby.

"Take your bluefish," explained Darby. "Pretty name, but what a vicious attacker! Or take the wolfeel—a nasty ocean-bottom patroller with sharp teeth! And who can overlook the sharks? They don't nibble, they just take tearing bites. And the ferocious manta rays. Need I continue? When these guys puncture that cable, the rays will have it easy."

The rays conferred and sent word they liked the idea because it spread the responsibility oceanwide instead of placing it all on their shoulders. "Will it work?"

"This project is getting out of hand," grumbled Heoo and Oola. "There are only two of us, and millions of so-called nibble fish. How will we ever supervise such an undertaking?"

"It will work, and who better than a whale to supervise a whale of a job?" asked Reginald Darby.

"I don't appreciate your attempt at English wit," Oola said.

But the word went forth by sonar, by gurgle, and by flap of fin. The response was overwhelming. It seemed that many creatures itched for the opportunity to become involved in something noble and purposeful. Not that their lives were boring. The life of a fish, although boring to a person because the fish can do so little, isn't dull for a fish because the fish isn't supposed to be anything other than what it is. So the response to the call for help arose not from dullness, but rather from a sense of the fullness – the fishiness, crabbiness, oysterness – in their lives, which they knew were in mortal danger.

They came in the hundreds, in the thousands. Oola and Heoo could hardly believe their prediction was true—in the millions. But the mighty whales need not have worried, for no supervision was needed. The whales had to act only as traffic cops, pointing to a large human nose two barracudas had painted on the hull of the cable, the target.

The nibble fish swam far deeper than they usually did. Various brightly lit lantern fish guided them so they easily found their way to the surface after making a jab.

Heoo and Oola had creatures shuttled to the deep in squads so there would be no long swimming in line. Big volunteers like the sharks and the barracudas struck the hardest, but every creature did the best with what it had.

There was only one incident: a shark hit the belly of a barracuda as she banked for an angle strike. The wounded 'cuda, thinking the hit intentional, immediately struck back. Soon other sharks and 'cudas joined in. The shellfish scattered.

Three rays watching the incident slithered between the combatants, and shocked several to their senses. Then everyone slowly returned to work. With one change: the 'cudas and sharks worked opposite shifts, the former by day, the latter by night; though at such depths, it was night twenty-four hours a day, or the day a twenty-four-hour night. Fish with surface contacts reported for shifts when the sun rose and when it set.

The careful spacing of creature types cooled tempers, and, eventually, the impossible happened. "A hole – a puncture!" came the cry. "Not a big one, but enough!"

Many fish stared in awe and disbelief, but Andy and several followers, their numbers swelled by recent arrivals, moved in quickly. The nibble fish hid as the rays poked their snouts, one at a time, first into the left painted nostril, then the right. Like a mini-heaven filled with lightning, the partially exposed and flooded wires inside the cable burst forth in an electrical shower.

Heoo yelled that the flooding would ruin the wires, and for the rays not to sacrifice themselves, but his warning was too late. The job had been done.

A huge cloud of black smoke poured from the sensitive wires, shot through with red and green streaks. It rippled noiselessly, but deadly, through the troubled waters, toppling the rays like duckpins caught in the backfire of their own un-

"A hole — a puncture," came the cry.

scheduled Fourth of July display. Many lay wounded and dying. Among them was Electric Andy.

Horrified by the carnage, the onlookers motioned the remaining rays to back off. "We want no more of you to die," said a bottlenose whale named Apso. "Come, let us help."

Turning their broad backs into stretchers and disregarding the shock value left in the wounded, Heoo, Oola, and a number of other whales carried the stricken rays to their distant homes to recover, or to die surrounded by their loved ones. The rays left behind a riddle for human inspectors to ponder: *How did a hole the size of two human nostrils develop in what should have been an airtight, impenetrable cable, severely crippling trans-Atlantic telephone contact?*

And just as important, could it happen again?

Orbiting satellites are the main source of communications these days, but the thick transatlantic cables were a good, reliable back-up in case an adversary neutralized or shot your satellites from the sky. Or were the satellites and GPS coordinating processes vulnerable to attack in some other way, on land or sea? Was anything totally secure?

As for Ampere Al, he was happy. His arch-rival, Electric Andy, was dead! He'd been elected the rays' new leader. Leader in a time of plenty! What luck! Now that the rays had succeeded bountifully, they would be awarded their booty—cushions, cushions, and more cushions. Ah, what a life!

Yet, for the first time in his life, Al was afraid. He had seen too much death. It was almost as though the buzzards had found a way to punish the rays for cooperating with the other fish, even though the buzzards were thousands of miles away, flying high.

The Buzzards' Scorecard

MAY 4

But the buzzards were not flying. They were on the ground, analyzing the situation, based on what they viewed as the biggest four of the many attacks that had by now taken place—just around the time that the terrorists were going to bomb Syria in order to draw Israel into the fray.

One win, one loss, and two draws.

Their reasons: the humans had won the battle to prevent a black-out of Omaha from spreading to the underground SAC headquarters. Low-flying pigeons hitting transformers had caused the black-out. But the humans lost a battle to prevent "real bugs" from destroying an enormous amount of computer tape at a Pakistani missile site, thus disrupting certain missile operations for several days while the Pakistanis scurried about for replacement tape.

The draws in these particular four battles against the humans were chemical spillage "unintentionally" caused by marauding foxes and other four-footed animals that nearly destroyed a French town where fissionable materials are produced, and a fire that raged out of control at a Chinese missile plant – nearly immobilizing firefighters and their equipment.

"Don't forget the nuclear power plant. Also a draw, I tell you!" a vulture screeched at a score-keeping buzzard, from the upper branch of a withered oak in Death Valley, California. This is where an assortment of vultures, buzzards, hawks, and condors, the bloodthirstiest of the bloodthirsty pillagers of carrion, had assembled to assess the situation.

"Humans fell like flies at Chernobyl, but there were only a few deaths, and they were all indoors, where we couldn't reach them," complained a hungry condor.

"But don't forget, many sheep in Lapland dying of radiation from Chernobyl," said a buzzard, strutting along the rocky ground, a bloody liver dangling from its mouth. "Them we could reach!"

"But the humans are becoming more cautious about nuclear plant construction," cried a second vulture. "So, it's a loss for us."

"The animals have made things worse. Humans capitulating. Humans weakening," said a wild-eyed hawk, pounding its short, rounded feathers. "Just watch! The terrorists will withdraw their threat to bomb the hell out of Nigeria," thus making a mistake over which country was to be bombed.

A third vulture looked over the score debris. A win was indicated by a bloody cut on a rocky ledge; a loss by a dried cow's skull; the draws by dog innards left to dry in the noonday sun.

"That unspeakably moral, upright elephant and his wretchedly decent cohorts must not be allowed to succeed!" said a kite.

"Not to worry," screamed an especially large, menacing vulture. "Canadian geese have more than once been mistaken for attacking Russian fighters. The experience so frightened them, they didn't know whether to listen to the elephant or us. I convinced them with this!" He held up the bloody head of a dead goose.

"Good, good!" cackled the third vulture. "That'll teach Awful Eddie to think he can lead all the animals and birds to safety!"

"He just wants absolute power."

"His concern masks greed."

"No safety, no refuge, no happiness!" shouted the fourth vulture, jumping up and down.

"The pigs have been highly successful in convincing

A third vulture looked over the score debris.

barnyard and non-barnyard passersby to stay clear. Gophers, chickens, woodchucks, and even some turtles are refusing to resist."

"We've convinced many the danger is not as real as the scare tactics have led them to believe."

"And indeed it's not," sniggered the Cooper hawk's mate, landing on the lower branch of a withered oak. "Such stuff and nonsense about demolishing the planet, or steering the earth off course. Merely because one or two hundred nuclear bombs may go off. And as for the threats of a burn-out of the ozone layer or a nuclear winter—why that's inedible rubbish!"

Nods all around.

"Meals, on the other hand," she salivated, "will be aplenty. The more wars, the more meals. The more meals, the more wars!"

"Fried brains."

"Radiated tongues."

"Pukey eyes."

"Dangling sexual organs."

"Roast livers."

"Stop, stop, stop!" said the buzzard with the skull. "You're making me hungry!"

"Tell that to the barn owls and bald eagles who're helping that despicable elephant!" said the second vulture.

"Why do they do that?" asked another vulture.

"Because they ridiculously consider this a beautiful planet," screeched a buzzard. To indicate the nuclear power plant uproar as a loss, he dropped the spare wolf's skull, picked clean of hide and meat, beside the cow's bleached bones. "But most owls and other birds mention the gallant pigs who were alienated because the other animals laughed at them during the Congress."

"Yes, we need not worry," said the first vulture, jumping from one dead branch to another. "Battles between animals and birds, with occasional defections, are nothing new. We've fought over turf and food since the dawn of time. It's old hat, I tell you—all old hat. Some eat flesh, others—can you imagine, are vegetarians. How they can stand those foul-smelling veggies and grain, I'll never know."

"Only death smells good!" said one old buzzard. Although limping with age, he still possessed a suitable lean and hungry look. "Which reminds me, how are the humans reacting?"

"As stupidly as ever, thankfully," said vulture number two. He sniffed the air for the scent of something dying. "They're much too crazy to realize this is one world or none. The only way they're going to survive us is to unite the globe. But we shan't tell them, shall we? Let them go on with their brainless wars, their juicy prejudices, and their destruction of thousands of species in the rain forests. All good news for us, by carrion!

Who doesn't hunger for their violence?" He glanced eagerly about; there was only one dissenter, the questioning buzzard.

"You didn't listen. I asked how humans were reacting to the war of the animals."

"You didn't ask that."

"Why you— " the old, but hearty, buzzard swooped to attack his younger opponent. But another buzzard and a hawk pushed the two apart. "We're here to plot, not to fight," cried the hawk. "Settle your differences in the desert, later."

"The humans have no idea the animals are attacking them," said the kite as the old buzzard and his adversary eyed each other warily. "People think no species but theirs has any brains, so when something goes wrong, they blame themselves, their stupid machines, or their gods, as in 'god-damnit.'" He stopped to gobble a fly that had flown too close. "Still, they do take precautions. The rupture of the trans-Atlantic telephone cables worries them. The mice in the grain stores upsets them. And the chemical spillage especially confuses them, because," he laughed, "contamination is so difficult to contain!"

"Oh, wonderful," cackled a middle-aged vulture. "Contaminate the water. Kill the drinkers. Let us dine. This is one time the plants won't help the humans survive as they did after the first great Congress eons ago."

"Oh, the plants are so docile and self-effacing, they'll probably help them again. But the only people with the knowledge to understand the food and medicinal values of the plants, and how they could feed the world ten times over, are the Indians, and they..." The kite rolled on the ground in a paroxysm of laughter "They..."

"What?" asked a falcon, leaning so far over his branch, it broke, sending him flying.

"They're...all...dead!" cackled the kite, kicking up the dust near a huge Saguaro cactus. "Killed off almost everywhere."

"Soon to be joined by more disgusting non-Indians!" squawked a buzzard. "If the slow death of acid rain doesn't get 'em, poisonous water will. And if the water doesn't, the big blow-up in the sky will! They haven't the brains to cooperate to save themselves."

"Ummmmm," said an old vulture, rubbing his belly, "I can hardly wait."

Delphic Rams Predict Disaster

MAY 6—11

What a cause for rejoicing! The dreaded day when the terrorists said they were going to attack Syria unless Syria would join in nuking Israel had come and gone—and no nuclear bombs had exploded. Animals and birds everywhere breathed a collective sigh of relief, even though Kazen had been unable to determine whether the terrorists had changed their minds about nuking Israel, or whether they had altered their thinking about the overall plan involving Syria. The rook kept delaying his intelligence gathering, complaining of stomach pains, withered wings, too much rain, or too little rain—anything to keep from flying to the heavily guarded Pakistani walls where he might risk losing his lunch over whatever awful carryings-on he might again overhear.

Kazen's friends tried to take up the slack, but they weren't as adept as the rook in finding those nice clean little places near partially open windows. When they flew to the window of the conference room where Kazen had listened, they complained of closed, curtained windows and wall-to-wall electrified sills, and even wild-eyed, mysterious looking men who stalked the grounds with machine guns.

Thus the creatures had no way to measure whether their efforts had forced the humans to have second thoughts, or whether their attacks had had no effect whatsoever.

But no matter. Why argue with success? Results were what counted. Not credit lines. And all the creatures who had participated in the revolt seemed happy with the results.

All but one.

Old Eddie.

"You seem unusually sullen tonight," said Gra'ma Elka to Eddie one evening after the keepers had closed up shop and gone home.

Around the zoo, the birds chirped about how disaster had been averted. And the hippo was bathing longer than usual in her enormous glee.

"I have a lot on my mind," said Old Eddie, waving his trunk absentmindedly into a mound of food. "And this hay tastes unusually dry." It wasn't the food or the revolt that bothered him. The revolt had gone well so far, but what worried him was a crucial bit of data he had withheld from everyone. He had concealed this information because the part he didn't understand scared him to death. And then there was the part that was, oh, golly...

"This hay isn't any more dry than usual," said Gra'ma Elka, scooping up a trunkful. "You're the only one who's dry—dry as a camel after a desert crossing. Now come to life and tell me what's wrong. It has to be something big. I know the symptoms."

Old Eddie looked at his mate, almost relieved. Why had he overlooked his natural confidant? But how could he confide this to her? Would she really understand?

"Really, Eddie. You're impossible," said Elka, as if reading his thoughts.

"Very well," sighed Eddie, "but I must take you back to Delphi, for that's the beginning of what is an olden tale."

"I'm not ignorant of the world, you know," said Elka, leisurely picking her huge teeth with a celery stalk. "I keep up with my aunts and uncles in Africa, don't forget."

"Ah, yes, well, they're not oracles," said Old Eddie, remembering a gossipy sea gull who had held Elka enthralled for hours with news of her very distant relatives. "This is a story of oracles or mediums known as the Pythia, women age fifty

Old Eddie looked at his mate, almost relieved.

to sixty, who lived apart from their husbands and dressed in young maidens' clothes. Sometimes they used ritual cakes in their ceremonies, but more often"—a hint of darkness crept into Eddie's deep voice—"they used a sacrificial animal that conformed to rigid physical standards."

"Ee-goo!" cried Elka, "you mean they raised their best and brightest for sacrifice?"

"Yes, but no one cared, because the Greek leaders, desperate to learn the outcome of projected wars or political actions, encouraged them. The oracle drank of a sacred spring, then entered the temple. There, she descended to an underground cell, mounted a tripod, ate the leaves of a laurel, and read the entrails of the slaughtered animals. Then in an abnormal state she uttered prophecies, almost never directly related to the inquirer, but transcribed by a priest in a highly ambiguous verse."

"Double ee-goo!" said Elka. "I sure don't want anyone reading my entrails!"

"You've hit upon something," whispered Eddie, so as not to wake the hippo sleeping nearby. "The prophecies were ambiguous because the oracles stupidly killed instead of studying and learning from living creatures."

"Incredible," said Elka, unable to continue eating. "But how do you know all this?"

"Because—"

"What?"

"Of some rams."

"Rams? What rams? There are no rams at this zoo. We have wildebeest, camels, and guanacos, but no male sheep!"

"Not here—in Delphi. In the great hills above the temple—where the animals for those bloody sacrifices lived. The descendants of those rams who lived there centuries ago still reside in those hills, quiet and undisturbed. Because of their connection with the ancient oracles, they claim they can forecast future events, the results of which they usually keep to themselves. But one day recently"—Eddie's voice grew ominous—"the rams foresaw something so out of the ordinary, so horrible, they couldn't contain it. Some birds heard it. They spoke to others and it crossed the ocean and came to rest in my ears."

A cold wind swept across the stall, sending dust into the air. Elka wrapped herself in her trunk. "What—what was it?

"The man who will push the nuclear button—"

"Thank Tusk, it won't be a woman!"

"Will be born sometime within the next year—"

"What's that you say?"

"Of an ordinary couple—"

"What?"

"Who live on—?"

"This can't be real!"

"A certain winding street, in a brick house with a broken

chimney and a weathercock facing north, surrounded by a white picket fence, in the town of Corrientes, Argentina."

"W-h-a-t?"

"The rams have not been able to determine the exact moment of conception."

"I should think not."

"But since they can't foresee events beyond their own lifetimes, and the heartiest Delphic ram dies at about age twenty-two or twenty-three—"

"What are you saying?"

"They expect the child born of this couple to push the button sometime in his early twenties. By that age he could be a member of the military, or associated with a terrorist group—"

"And poof! There goes the National Zoo," squawked an eavesdropping sparrow, looking around as if for the last time.

"This isn't the only zoo in the world," said another sparrow. "I once had a delicious meal from a rhino's barrel at the wonderful Pittsburgh Zoo."

"You fool, there won't be any zoos left! Nothing left—period."

"Stop it," Elka shouted, swatting at one of the sparrows with her trunk, sending it flying. Whirling, she nearly knocked Eddie for a loop. "You fool," she said, shaking her head furiously, "have you done nothing to prevent this conception from taking place?"

"Prevent—what?" asked Eddie, regaining his footing, but not his mental balance. "What ? What are you talking about? Do what?"

"The conception? What have you done to prevent it?"

"I don't know what you are talking about. I—"

"Braa-cha!" Elka trumpeted, awakening the whole zoo.

Birds and small animals came running, flying and crawling from all directions to see who was being called an idiot at three o' clock in the morning. And why?

They soon found out and began to bombard Eddie with criticism.

Old Eddie took the criticism, but he didn't like it. And he was simply flabbergasted to learn the impossible was possible. How is it possible? he asked himself, shifting his weight from one leaden foot to the other.

"It's as possible as the bubonic plague, caused by flies and rats," Elka reminded him. "As possible as trichinosis spread by pigs. As possible as malformed babies, caused by our unsung friends," – she screwed up her face in an expression of disgust – "the viruses and the bacteria."

A shudder passed through the audience.

Eddie looked at Elka, an alarmed expression on his usually placid face. Surely Elka wasn't thinking of calling them for help. But from the sound of it, she was! Everyone knows that viruses and bacteria can be used to sustain life, but they can also be deadly.

"As I recall," said Elka, looking at Eddie, "you once told me that in the beginning days of Earth, the viruses and bacteria left man alone. There were no diseases, no ailments. But when people sought supremacy and domination, resulting in the falling out between man and his environment, the 'vir-bacs'—the alliance of viruses and bacteria—joined the rebellion. 'Man will hurt us,' they said, 'so we'll strike back—with cancer, TB, the plague, malaria, diabetes, and a thousand others.'"

"I also recall telling you that the vir-bacs had a sense of humor, too. They get quite a kick out of the common cold, where many different viruses – over a hundred – team up so that man finds it impossible to combat it. The viruses love to hang around to hear the superior, high falutin' humans sneezing, wheezing, coughing, sniveling, and pill-popping. When the viruses hear a comment such as 'We put a man on the moon, but we can't defeat the common cold,' they titter – microscopically, of course – and often leave and let the person with the cold recover just like that!"

"We must get their help," said Elka. "Dangerous or not. Some of them have already helped us in the attack on the nuclear power plant."

"That was much different, and less dangerous." said Eddie. "I forbid it."

"Why?"

"We've used them once and got away with it. We can't push our luck. If we do, they may consider us as haughty as humans, and turn against animals nearly as often as people."

"Don't I know full well what you mean? Don't forget I lost one child to pneumonia, and another to dirty, brackish water before zoo days," said Elka, a hardness to her shiny black eyes.

"They were my children, too," said Old Eddie, sadly.

"Of course, I'm sorry, you wonderful, big old duffer you," said Elka, rubbing a leg against her mate's rubbery hide. "I know the hours you sat up with me, trying to save them." They looked at each other with the expressions of two creatures who had passed through the fire of experience and grown together from it. "We will be careful, I assure you."

"We'd better be," he said as ten or fifteen fearful creatures gathered around them.

"Very well. We'll send emissaries to the vir-bacs," said Elka. "In the meantime, while we're waiting to hear from them, we've important spade work to do."

"You mean digging for roots?" asked a chestnut-colored chipmunk named Rutabaga. "I love to dig for tubers, especially the ripe ones, like potatoes in season, or beets."

"No, I don't mean tubers," said Elka. "I mean we must nail down..."

"One doesn't nail tubers," said Rutabaga. "One digs them with one's paws."

"Will someone please take this chipmunk for a drink of water?"

"But I'm not thirsty," protested the brown and white furry creature.

"You'll return refreshed," called Elka, as a squirrel named Ari edged the objecting chipmunk towards the gate.

"Now the rest of you gather 'round," said Elka, grateful that Eddie didn't seem to object, at least for now. "I'll explain what we have to do, and how."

According to animal lore, nothing much had ever happened in Corrientes, an impoverished town on the Parana River, except for one year when a dog catcher was bitten three times – by the same dog. That dog, a snappy brown and white fox terrier named Juanita, became a hero to the local animal populace from that day on. It wasn't surprising when Juanita was chosen unanimously to supervise the animals' local intelligence-gathering operation.

Juanita, who claimed "My bite is worse than my bark," had teams of informants on the dusty, dirty roads and in the trees, within minutes of receiving her commission. Forty-eight hours later, the sketchy picture of the couple that the rams had provided had been amply enlarged.

The information was flown as quickly as possible to the National Zoo by bird relay teams, the last hundred miles of which were covered by a cowbird named Lulubell. Though fired at with buckshot from a farmer's gun in North Carolina and attacked by a hungry fox as she ate dinner in a cornfield near Sperryville, Virginia, Lulubell managed to arrive safe and sound at the zoo in mid-May.

Elka, Eddie, and the other members of the nightly council waited patiently as the famished Lulubell ate a hastily arranged meal contributed by the Rock Creek Park crows.

"I suppose you'd first like to hear about the prospective husband," said Lulubell between bites of seed and nuts.

"Or the wife," said Elka.

The bird scratched her head.

Seeing the bird needed some direction, Eddie said, "Begin with the husband."

"Not much to say," said the bird, as if having forgotten everything somewhere between the buckshot and the fox. "Oh, the husband – yes, he's young. Twenty-four or twenty-five, I believe, with sandy brown hair, fair skin, and a wart on his big right toe—"

"How can you possibly know that?"

"Can't say for sure," said Lulubell, nibbling some nuts. Then, as if some computer program had been activated: "Wart, husband, big toe, of course, two witnesses, a bluejay named Thomasina and a cardinal named Frecco."

"Very thorough," cawed Ingabell, Lulubell's cowbird cousin, also a member of the zoo roundtable. "Please continue."

"The father—"

"He's already a father?" said an ashen-faced gopher.

"Excuse me. Slip of the tongue. He and his mate have no children—yet."

"And for the world's sake, better never have," said Elka. "If the rams are six months or a year off in their forecast, nothing can be done in time. There's no way we can justify killing a child, no matter what the prognosis, though the viruses wouldn't hesitate a minute."

Eddie nodded. "And we can't even trip, attack, or frighten the woman into a miscarriage. It's too disgusting for animals to consider."

"But we can prevent a pregnancy," said Elka. "That's more abstract, more conceptual, and justifiable. Especially because the existence of everyone's child is at stake."

"The end justifying the means," said Eddie pensively.

"Perhaps, but only in an isolated instance, and then not without strong social and moral considerations. We cannot claim to be upset about the falling out between man and the environment if we're insensitive to the delicate balance between every living thing—even every conceptualized being."

The crescent moon scudded past a cloud. Lulubell disgustedly spat out a shell that contained no nut. "They don't make nuts the way they used to," she complained.

"The husband..." Lulubell continued, as Elka pushed more seed her way. "The husband is never seen to have any contact with animals or birds, and is therefore considered insensitive and dumb. But he seems to have made an uncommonly good choice for a mate," Lulubell said between chews. "The wife often places a saucer of milk on her porch for stray cats. She maintains a bird bath and feeder at full capacity. Many people have both but let the water run dry and the feeder remain empty—and get this—" the plump little bird preened her feathers, "she even walks around anthills instead of squishing them!"

"So the woman is decent. But what has to be done must be done," said Elka. Great ivory, she thought, I sound like Eddie in one of his confused moments. But that was neither here nor there. The vir-bacs had agreed to help, no matter how nasty the assignment, and there was no more excuse for delay.

The Viruses & Bacteria

MAY 13–27

Two weeks later, reporters and television cameramen from Buenos Aires swarmed about a small house at 123 Calle Plumas in Corrientes to report what one journalist called "an unusual outbreak of swine flu in this remote northern town. The unusual thing about this rare disease is that it has struck not one, but both members of the same *casa*, a young couple married only six months."

A group of pigs, who had never heard of swine flu and certainly never suspected the dread disease lay dormant in their bodies, shook violently when given the news, but then snorted delightedly when hearing that the same awful viruses had left their bodies forever and were now directed at more deserving targets. Called H1N1 by scientists and "Beep," "Blop," "Bop," "Bo-Beep," and the like by each other, viruses—the undercover operatives of the submicroscopic world—disappeared into what to them were enormous openings in the young couple's pores, respiratory systems, and stomachs, never to be seen again.

Sometime later, according to a wandering mouse, the couple's doctor attributed the runny noses, protracted coughing, and high fever to "severe cases of the flu." He advised the couple to rest quietly in bed, but when the symptoms worsened and new ones developed, the couple's cousin, a colonel in an Argentine hospital, had them flown to Cordoba. There, an internist diagnosed the true nature of the couple's ailment. And there they stayed. Swine flu was serious!

"They'll not conceive in that hospital," hooted an owl named Grot, who had seen the couple whisked away by ambulance. "No, no, no."

"No what, no what?" chirped José, a blue-jay, popping up and down on Grot's observation post, the limb of a scraggly pin oak in the stricken couple's small but well-tended backyard.

"No sex, no sex, no sex," Grot hooted loudly, his furry brown head swiveling 155 degrees alternately right and left with each singsong repetition of "No sex."

Then one evening, Grot awoke with alarm. Lights shone from the window of the house where the young couple lived.

He heard voices and laughter. The hospital stay had not lasted. The couple had come home. He flew closer to the house and looked in the bedroom window. "They're at it again! They're at it again!" he screamed, sounding the alarm. Soon a score of birds landed on the branch beside him.

"What to do, to do, to do," croaked Grot, his black eyes widening.

The branch of the tree sagged with so much fowl weight, but it was the only branch that permitted a perfect, unobstructed view of the couple's bedroom at the rear of the four-room stucco house.

"Stop it, stop it, stop it!" caterwauled the owl.

The other birds looked at each other, puzzled. What was that owl squawking about? The sagging branch, everyone's sagging hopes, or the sagging bed?

José stared with fascination at the humans' intertwined limbs. "Why does she allow him to climb over her like a horse?" he asked. "We birds wouldn't tolerate that. It's so un-birdlike."

"It's so un-owl like, too, but that's not the point," said Grot, feathers ruffled. "We must stop this nonsense—forevermore, forevermore, forevermore."

Raven or not, Grot sent word immediately to the zoo.

Elka put "Plan B" into action right away.

Several days later the wife contracted chicken pox. The husband was diagnosed as suffering from a pre-mononucleotic

"They're at it again! They're at it again!" he screamed, sounding the alarm.

condition. In addition, both now battled diarrhea, skin eruptions, and unaccustomed headaches. The husband was hospitalized again. A day later his wife followed.

The neighborhood where the young couple lived again buzzed with reporters and cameramen, interviewing people about what the animal and bird species heard one journalist describe as "the plague of bad luck that's haunting this young señor and señora."

Neighbors interviewed for the camera – indeed, it was the first time some of them had seen a television camera – attributed the ill fortune of the couple to a variety of causes.

From a priest: "They're fallen-away Catholics, and have strayed from the Lord."

From a mother of ten, who prided herself on being the best cook in town: "The obvious result of not cooking their meat long enough before dinner. I told them time and time again, but they were too proud to listen."

From a neighborhood shopkeeper: "Their cousin, the colonel, wanted them to live in Buenos Aires near him, but they said no, they prefer to live near cattle ranches. Now, que horrible! They paid the price for family disobedience."

Only a gentle, elderly man, who fed turtles by the occasionally turbulent and overflowing Parana River, expressed any sympathy for the young couple's sufferings. "It is sad, but they will get better," he said.

After the reporters had gone, leaving more than one hedge broken, the animal and bird surveillance team had little to do. Grot, though conscious of the irony, took a break to start raising a family of his own, but he was careful to choose a little-used barn in a quiet meadow not far away from 123 Calle Plumas, so if he had to return suddenly he would be within hailing distance. The hailing came one night a few weeks later, when he was summoned to a meeting at a certain fence post midway between Calle Plumas and his barn home.

Much to Grot's surprise, he was met not by a delegation of birds and animals, but by a lone, mangy alley cat, who on top of everything else was half an hour late.

"Who, who, who – oo are you-oo-oo?" hooted Grot. "No-ooo, I won't talk to you. This is not proper."

"My name, she eez Isadora," said the cat with a distinctly French accent. "I was sent with news. The bad news is that ze husband and wife are back home. The good news is that ze husband has lost his job at a nearby sheet metal factory."

"Why is that good news? People are supposed to love work. The fools."

"I assure you, these ees good news," said Isadora, her hackles rising. "I purposely went without food for a week so the wife could take pity on me when I show up at the door. *Alors*! She and her mate are just finishing *petit dejeuner*, and they are arguing. She say, 'If you hadn't called ze boss so often from ze hospital, he wouldn't have'—how you say? 'fi-yard you.' Ze husband yells at her: 'You don't know what you're talking about. The economy, she is bad, and the boss needs no excuse to fi-yar anyone.'"

"So?"

"Then ze husband yell: 'I could be at death's door, and my boss wouldn't give a hoot!'"

"Wouldn't give a hoot?" Grot swiveled his head. "Are you sure the human used that word? I wonder if he suspects I've been watching him?"

"I doubt very much if he knows you watch him," said the feline, patting her stomach. "Now if you don't mind, I going to get myself ze good hot meal and sleep for a week. The wife, she give me only scraps—ze cold scraps."

"Wait!" cried Grot. "What about their mating?"

"What about it?"

"Are they, or aren't they?"

"I told you zey were arguing and angry wiz each other."

"So?"

"So people who argue are too angry to make ze love."

"But even angry people can make up," the owl screeched.

Ah, that is what occurs, thought the cat, as she slinked away. *Animals are like people. Starve yourself for a week, bring 'em good news, and they're still not satisfied. Zey always want more. Let them get a German cat as a spy next time. He'll give them so many details, he'll harangue them for a month. And zey still won't understand what happened!"*

All the happiness and praise was indeed forgotten, when Grot, just to be on the safe side, glided by the old pin oak later that night. His feathers stood on end at what he saw through the bedroom window.

"Ack, ack, ack! The humans! They're at it again!" screeched Grot, spreading alarm up and down the land.

And sure enough, the following morning, three hastily assembled squirrels watched the husband leave the house, lunch bucket in hand, a kiss on the cheek from his spouse. He'd found a new job; they had indeed made up.

Elka wallowed in her mud hole, attempting to drown her worries. What to do? Kill the couple? Would anything short of death stop them? She wondered what to ask the vir-bacs to do next. Then a rhino in an adjoining pool, who until now had contributed nothing to the revolt, made a suggestion that was as wise as it was unexpected. How such a dainty water creature could come up with such a super idea she didn't know, but she decided to gamble on it.

On the following night, as the young couple embraced tenderly, a tiny lime green bug inched his way up the shaking queen-size bed. It was rough going for the diminutive creature with many feelers, and several times he almost lost his footing. But he hung on and finally crossed the blue silk sheets to the pillows. There, he paused to catch his breath before getting to the business at hand, which he was more than glad to do. He had no use for humans. They called him a stink bug. Why, he didn't know. To himself he smelled just fine – like a bug ought to smell. Before he had time to plan his attack, the wife turned her head and spotted him.

"Get that disgusting thing away from me," she yelled.

The husband, not seeing the bug, gasped, moaned, and shrank back from his mate, landing on his behind with a thud on the hardwood floor. And none too soon. The woman threw up all over the sheets, just missing the stink bug as he scrambled down the side of the bed as fast as his six tiny feet could carry him.

A fly-on–the-wall reported the incident as "a violent eruption."

"Ridiculous," said a non-media mouse, striking a blow for journalistic integrity. "You'd describe a shaking leaf as an earthquake. Everyone knows the human female always vomits when she sees a horrible bug."

"She wasn't vomiting," said another fly-on-the-wall. "She was merely giving the male species as hard a time as he tried to give her."

"Why must you always fly in the face of reason?" complained the mouse.

Though the fly was off base, the stink bug had done the job. The husband had "bugged off," taking with him a suitcase, an iPod, and a pair of boxing gloves.

And as far as periodic surveillance by animal and bird species could tell in the coming months, he never moved back.

The battle to stop a birth at 123 Calle Plumas had succeeded.

Juanita, the brown and white fox terrier rejoiced and didn't bite any dog catchers for an entire year.

Apparently the danger was past. But Old Eddie knew differently. The need to prevent the birth of the human who could destroy the world, coming as it did after the terrorist threat, had convinced him that the threat of disaster generated by the humans was never-ending.

The animals could not become complacent. Their plans must be updated and attacks carried out regularly. The issues were more complex, human attitudes more difficult to change than originally imagined, and staying power would be mandatory if they were to survive. And he must convince the animals of their ongoing mission: eternal vigilance.

And so he did.

Watchfulness became their constant state.

Epilogue

One could continue to recount the tales of bravery and innocence on the part of the insects, birds, fishes, reptiles, and four-footed beasts.

Everyone blamed the crisis that came in the wake of Katrina on a hurricane. True, the hurricane was a force of nature. So too were the small animals who bit and chewed through the levees for five years, hoping that minor flooding would confuse the humans into rethinking their priorities.

Everyone knew about global warming. But did they know that many polar bears could have withstood the onslaught for five or ten more years? Instead, they jumped ice floe to ice floe to get into the open sea as a way of *really* alerting the humans to global warming—and hence the need to save the planet. The polar bears sacrificed themselves and their families.

President George W. Bush often exhibited a nervous tic in his eye. It was a tick all right. In fact, several different ticks over a period of time. Anything to confuse the man who was already confused.

And a massive oil spill nearly destroyed the Gulf of Mexico, killing millions of sea creatures, but making humans once again realize that they can't be careless with the planet. Contrary to the animals' policy of keeping casualties to a minimum, the loss of life as a result of the oil spill—especially among sea creatures— was staggering, and the environment was colossally damaged.This, Old Eddie realized, had been an enormous mistake. So he replaced the turtle generals with a new set of generals and instructed them to be far more careful in future attacks. But an error, even a horrendous one, only meant a change in direction, not a change in purpose.

At this point, it is sufficient to say that the war continues.

Humans continue to destroy animals, birds, fish, and insects—far more than the creatures could inadvertently destroy themselves.

So the creatures fight back, despite the objectives of the buzzards.

They fight back—in ways that humans do not yet understand.

About the Author

DAVID L. LEVY

David L. Levy is a pioneer in the field of children's rights. In 1985, Levy cofounded the National Council for Children's Rights, later renamed the Children's Rights Council. As President of CRC, Levy directed the Board of Trustees to strengthen families and reduce the trauma of divorce to children through supporting legislation and programs that favor shared parenting (joint custody), mediation, access/parenting time (visitation), and financial and emotional child support. Levy received a Lifelong Achievement Award for his "untiring efforts on behalf of the Children of America" from the National Child Support Office in September 2000. Levy and

CRC received the 1996 Distinguished Service to Children award from Parents Without Partners International, and the 1996 Legislative Achievement award from the National Parents' Day Coalition.

Levy graduated from the University of Florida Law School and is a member of the Washington, D.C., and U.S. Supreme Court bars.

A noted author, Levy has written numerous articles on the subject of child custody and divorce mediation, which have been published in prominent legal journals as well as noted general interest publications. He was named one of The 25 Most Influential People in the Lives of our Children by *Children's Health* magazine, October 2009 issue.

David is the author of the forthcoming title *Creating a Safer Society: 10 Ways to Help Children Avoid Crime, Drugs, Teenage Pregnancy, and Gangs* due to be published in 2011. He is also the author of the novel *The Potomac Conspiracy* and was editor of *The Best Parent is Both Parents: A Guide to Shared Parenting in the 21st Century*.

Passionate about the environment and the preservation of life, both human and animal, David hopes this novel will help in some small way to galvanize greater efforts to save this planet for the benefit of *all* its inhabitants.

He lives with his wife in the Washington, D.C., metro area. He has two grown children.

About the Illustrator

This book was conceived in the mid-1980s. At some point, a very talented artist created pen-and-ink illustrations of the various characters within the manuscript. The only signed illustration is "Eddie the Elephant." The signature mark on Eddie reads, "SAVAGE ©," and is not dated.

Every attempt has been made to research and contact the illustrator, SAVAGE, prior to the publishing of this book, but those efforts were unsuccessful.

So, it is with some sadness that this book, with such great illustrations, goes to press without being able to properly acknowledge this great illustrator.

Salute, illustrator SAVAGE.

May your gift live on through our publication.

Acknowledgments

As a book develops over a twenty-five year period, it owes much to those who kept the idea alive for this book.

I am indebted to my wife, Ellen Dublin Levy, who read the first draft in the mid-1980s, and edited the changes I made every five years or so. My wonderful sister, Carol Levy, is always supportive. I also thank my first wife, Ginger Carey, for helping me publish my first novel and for continuing to encourage my creative writing.

I thank book agent Joyce Wright, who always had faith in this book.

I am grateful to Munro Meyersburg, who realized that the

book needed another update after 9/11, and to his brother Rich, my terrific friend, who lent moral support along the way.

I very much appreciate Harvey Walden, editor extraordinaire, who says he developed his talent from his dad, who was once an editor of *New Yorker* magazine.

I am delighted with Lary Holland, who introduced me to Nina and Brian Taylor, of Pneuma Books, who are truly outstanding book producers.

"Savage," who prepared the wonderful illustrations for this book in the mid-80s, and whose whereabouts are currently unknown, has earned my gratitude.

I of course thank my children, Justin and Diana, who appreciate the outdoors, ride bicycles, and take environmental matters seriously.

I thank the eighth graders at Hyattsville Middle School in Maryland and their teacher, David Moore, to whom I read portions of this book.

And I could not conclude this page without a reference to all the animals, birds, and fishes with whom we share this marvelous, imperiled Earth.

ABOUT THE TYPE USED IN THIS BOOK

The titles and the body of this book are typeset in *Mrs. Eaves*, designed by Zuzana Licko for Emigré in 1996 as a reprise of the classic Transitional typeface *Baskerville*, crafted in 1757, under the direction of master type designer and famed printer John Baskerville. The name, Mrs. Eaves, comes from John Baskerville's maid, Sarah Eaves, who became his wife after the death of her first husband. Baskerville was originally designed for use in a Bible. The beauty and versatility of Mrs. Eaves allow for its use as both a display and a body typeface.

The Native American Legend dingbat is typeset in *Caravan LH3* by the Linotype foundry.

The Rook dingbat is typeset in *Animal* by Fontographer.

Cover & interior design, typesetting, and page layout by Brian Taylor, Pneuma Books, LLC.

LaVergne, TN USA
19 September 2010
197509LV00002B/1/P